Memoirs of

Sherlockian Realism:

Sherlock Holmes Cartoons

from a warped mind

Volume 4

By

Don Hobbs

Paperback ISBN 978-1-78705-863-7

Published by MX Publishing
335 Princess Park Manor, Royal Drive,
London, N11 3GX
www.mxpublishing.co.uk

Cover design by Brian Belanger

To

The Crew of the Barque Lone Star, the Dallas area Sherlock Holmes Society, ran in the competent hands of Mr. Steve Mason

Contents

221 Sherlockian Aesthetic Realism drawings by Don Hobbs with a canonical explanation accompanying each.

Foreword

This all started in the fall of 2011 when my wife Joyce and I stumbled across the Napoleon Museum during our "Roaming Rome" vacation. Inside there was an art exhibit by Chiam Koppleman, the American artist known for his works of Aesthetic Realism. The exhibit was entitled 'Napoleon Enters New York' and it featured drawings and paintings of Napoleon in various unfamiliar settings, like entering Coney Island or riding alligators. His Bicones hat and his epaulette-coat were always present in the pictures and something about this exhibit struck a chord with me. Immediately I knew I had to start my own series of drawings. Thus was born Aesthetic Sherlockian Realism. The pipe and deerstalker replace the epaulettes and Bicones. The Master replaces the Emperor. So enjoy my artistic adventure where the game is afoot.

Sherlock Holmes
Likes Sixty Minutes

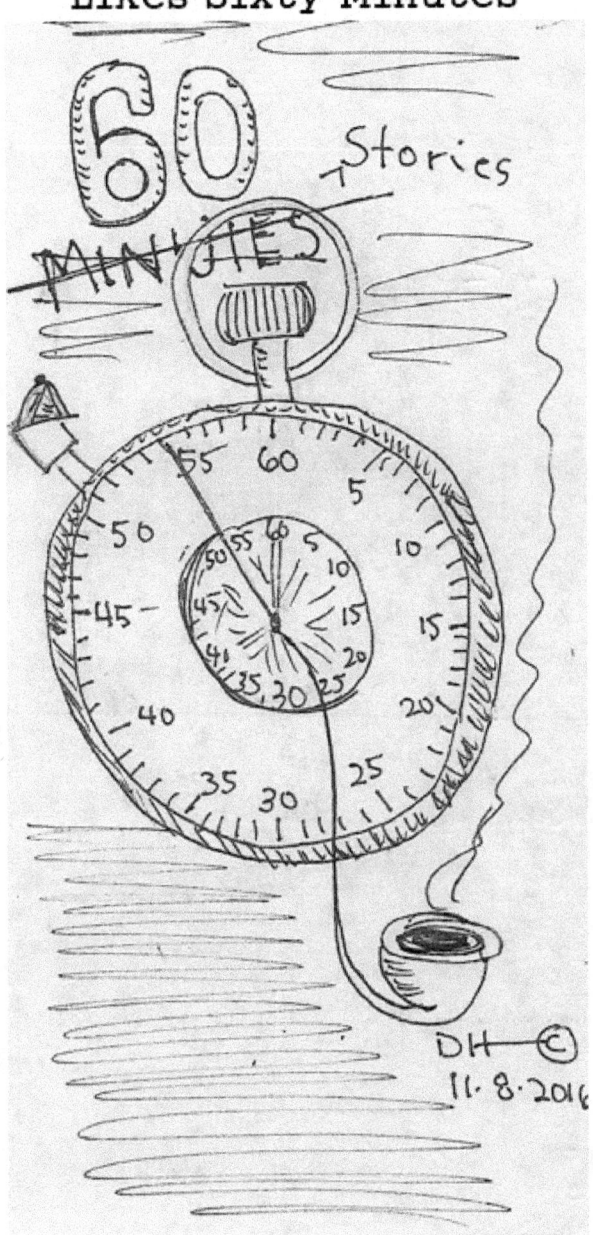

60 ~~MINUTES~~ Stories

DH © 11·8·2016

"…To be with a man for an hour is unpleasnt…" ABBE

Sherlock Holmes
Visits Bangar, ME

"...I picked up a battle axe..." MUSG

Sherlock Holmes
In Maine

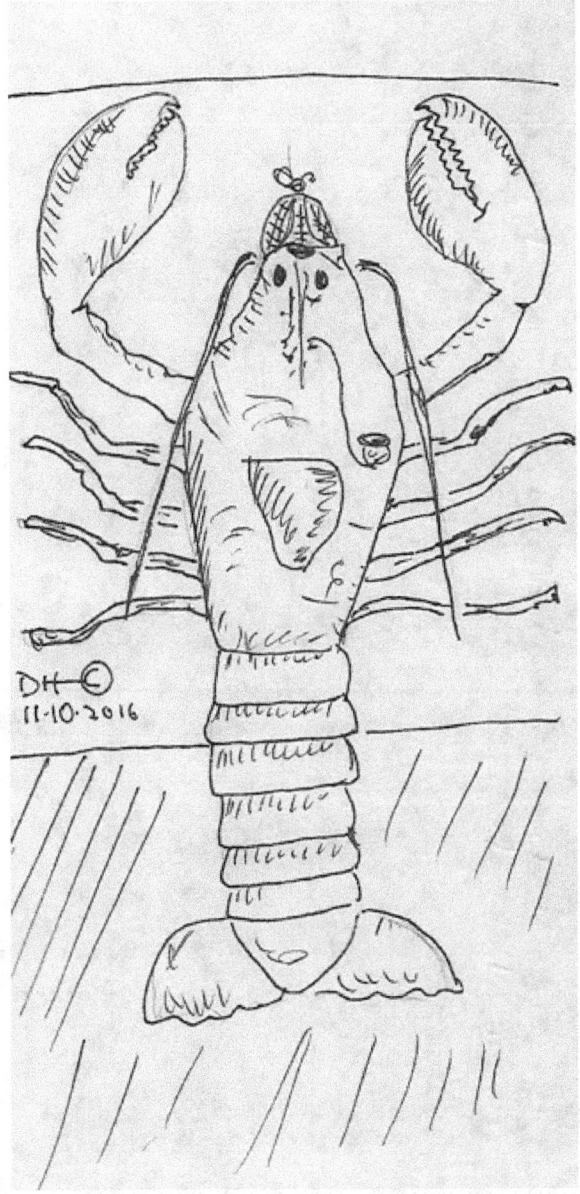

"...He is as brave as a bull dog and as tenacious as a lobster..." REDH

Sherlock Holmes
Feeds the Birds

"...Fine birds they are, too..." BLUE

Sherlock Holmes
Will Miss Leon Russell

"...Leon..." DEVI

Sherlock Holmes
Pinball Wizard

"...showed a thin white slit of ball beneath..." STOC

Sherlock Holmes
Crossing

"...he had rather be a free crossing sweeper in
New York than a large mine owner under..." VALL

Sherlock Holmes
Enjoys Florence
Street Art

"...I found myself in Florence..." EMPT

Sherlock Holmes Suffers From a Toothache

"...his second tooth on the left-hand side..." STOC

Sherlock Holmes
Loves Artoo Detoo

"...You are too timid..." BLUE

Sherlock Holmes
Cuts the Mustard

"...so he is always as keen as mustard..." COPP

Sherlock Holmes
Bottle Opener

"...Why, a Yankee crook would be into it with a can-opener..." LAST

Sherlock Holmes is a
Dak Prescott Fan

"...when the Prescott outfit was discovered..." 3GAR

Sherlock Holmes
Emoji

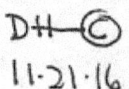

11-21-16

"...I left him full of the image of his magnificent
intellect babbling like a foolish child..." DYIN

Sherlock Holmes
Is the Pilgrim's Pride

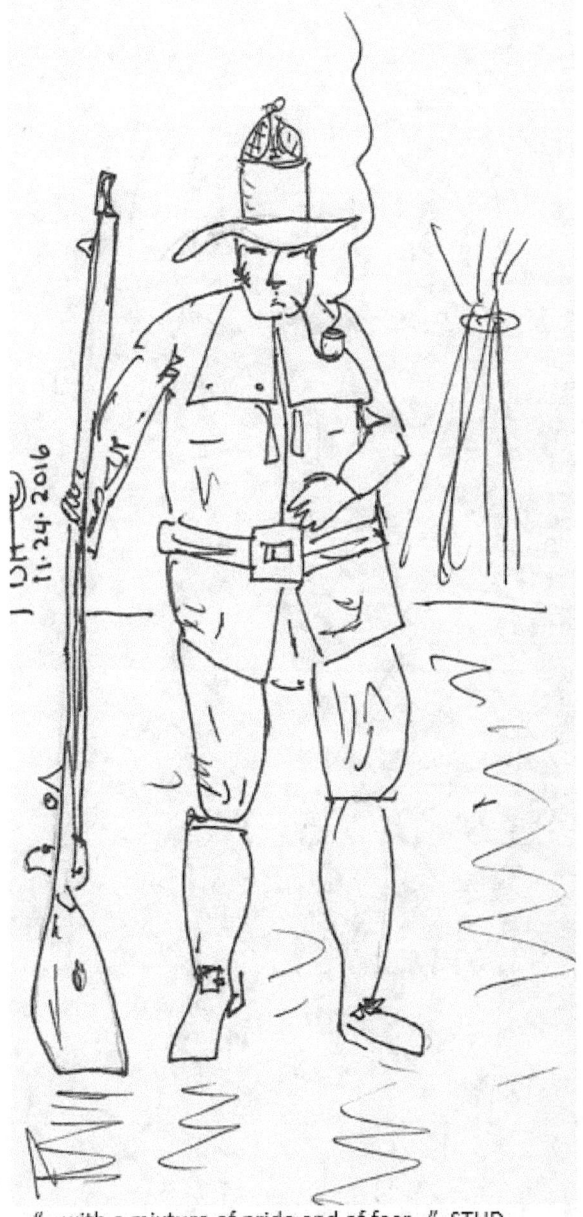

"...with a mixture of pride and of fear..." STUD

Sherlock Holmes
Folk Art

"...He could evaluate my simple art..." BLAN

Sherlock Holmes is a
Visits Wyoming

"...the defiles which he had already traversed on
horseback..." STUD

Sherlock Holmes Cleans Up At the Box-Office

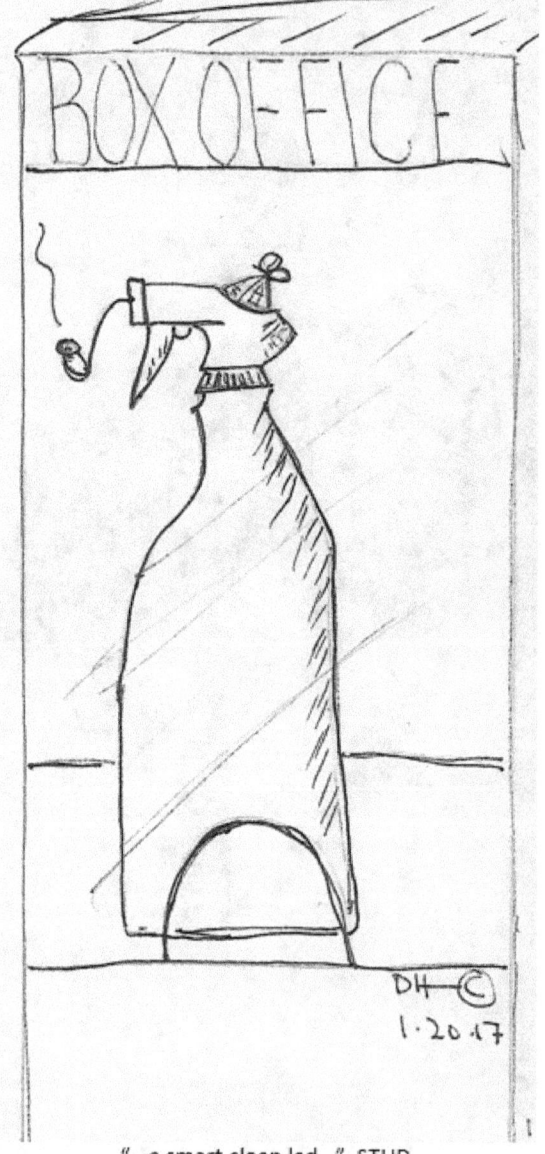

"...a smart clean lad..." STUD

Sherlock Holmes
Is Spot On

"...I was on the spot..." BLAC

Sherlock Holmes
Is Always Unique

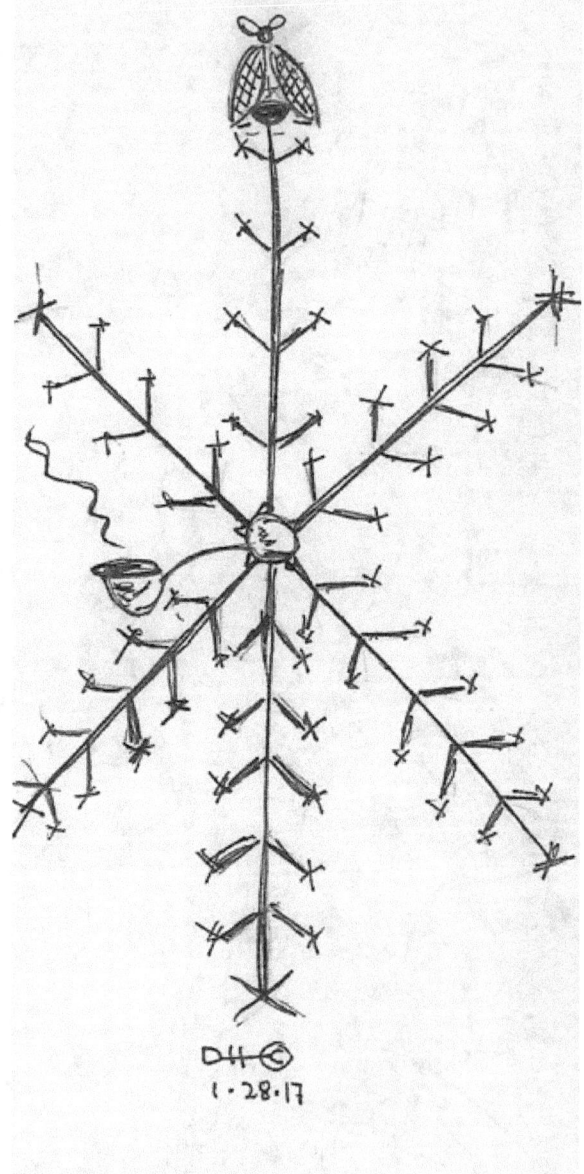

"...pressed right through the snow..." BERY

Sherlock Holmes
A Candal in Bohemia

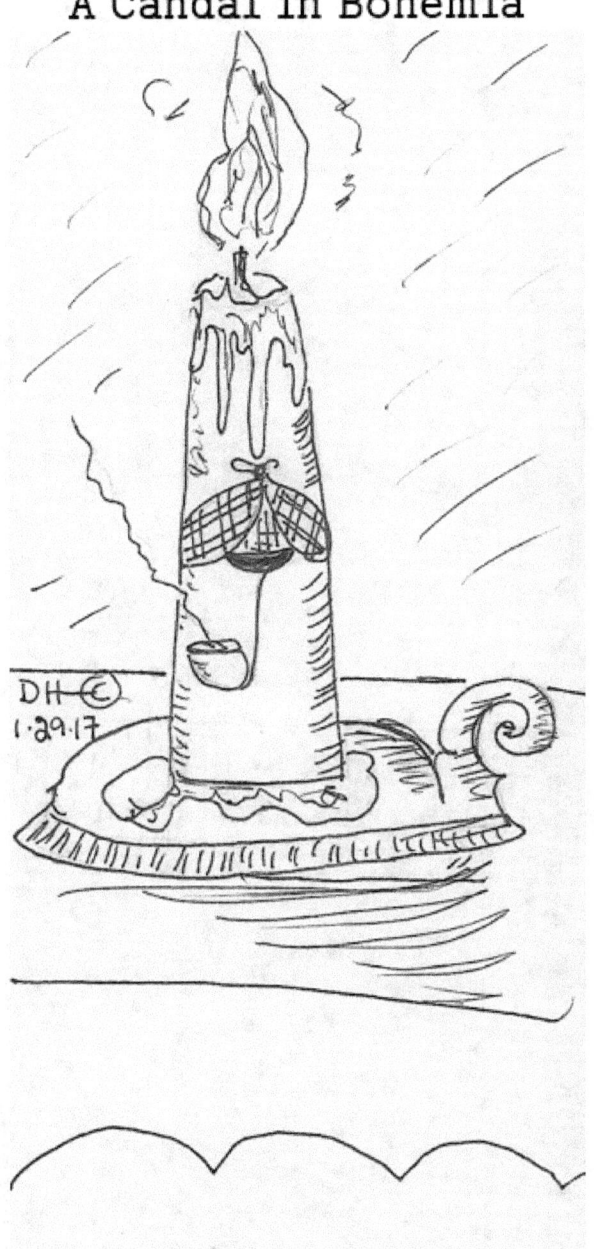

"...The candal shows us that..." VALL

Sherlock Holmes
Visits Toronto, Again

"...this young stranger from Canada..." HOUN

Sherlock Holmes
Visits Downunder

DH (c)
2.26.17

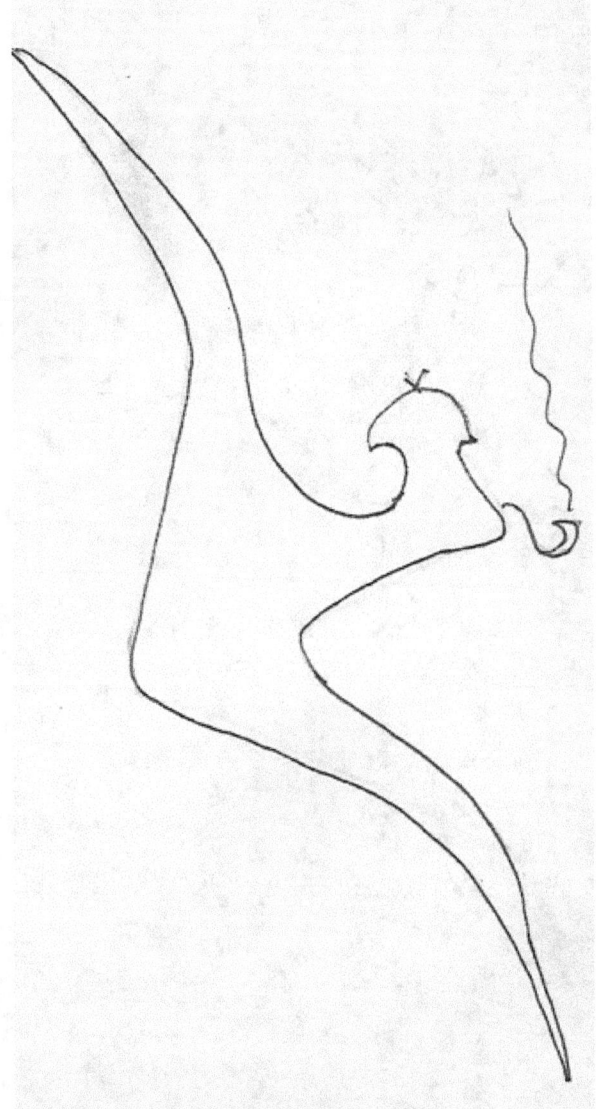

"...bound for Australia..." GLOR

Sherlock Holmes
Visits Sweetwater, TX

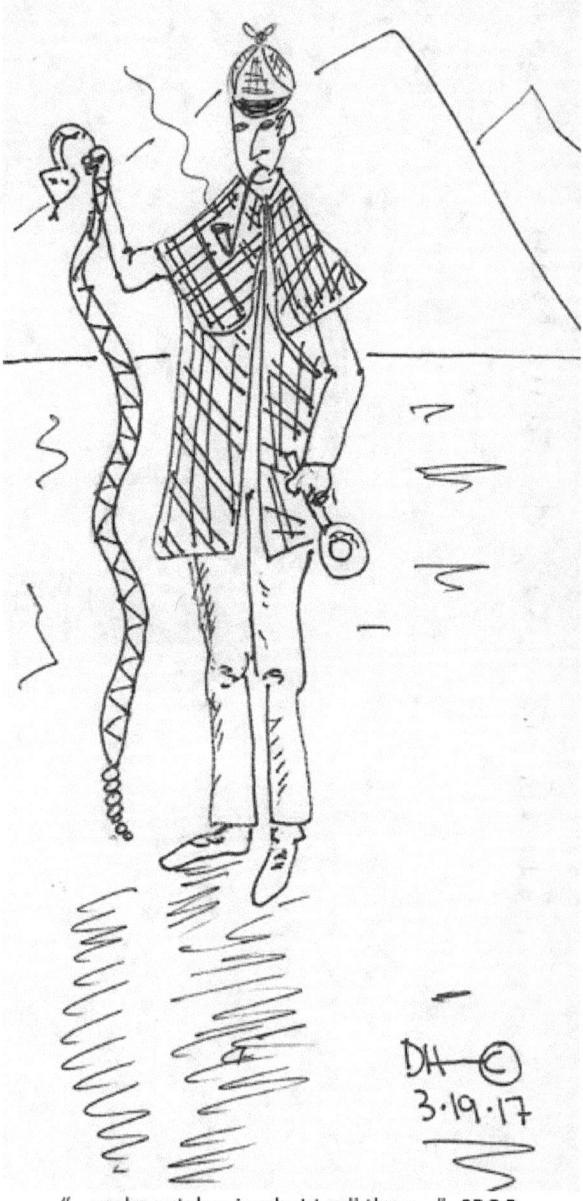

"...snake catcher is what I call them..." CROO

Sherlock Holmes
Never Mails It In

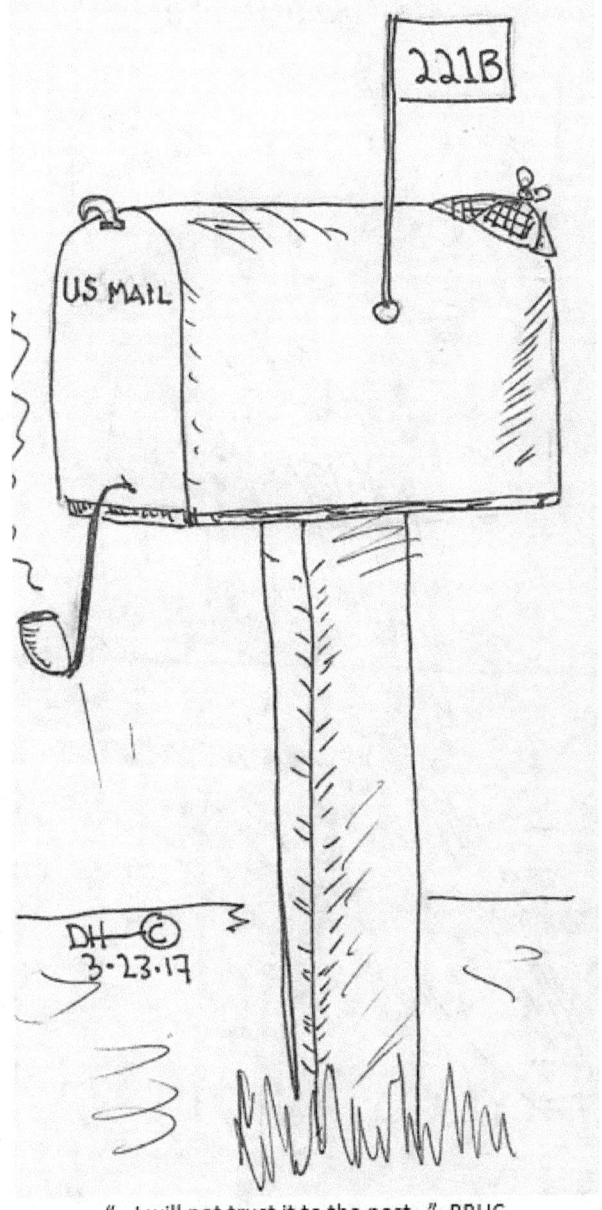

"...I will not trust it to the post..." BRUC

Sherlock Holmes Disguised as a Mockingbird

"...with a kind of mocking laugh..." CARD

Sherlock Holmes
Perfers Coffee

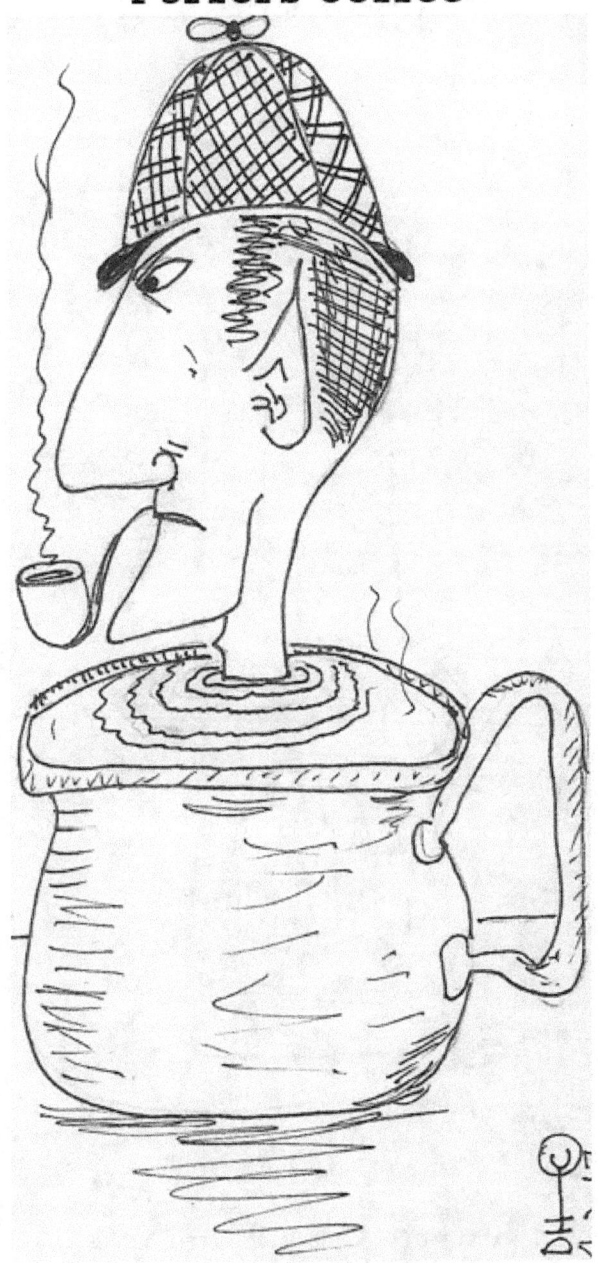

"...he was with a cup of coffee..." BERY

27

Sherlock Holmes
Disgushed As a Chimenia

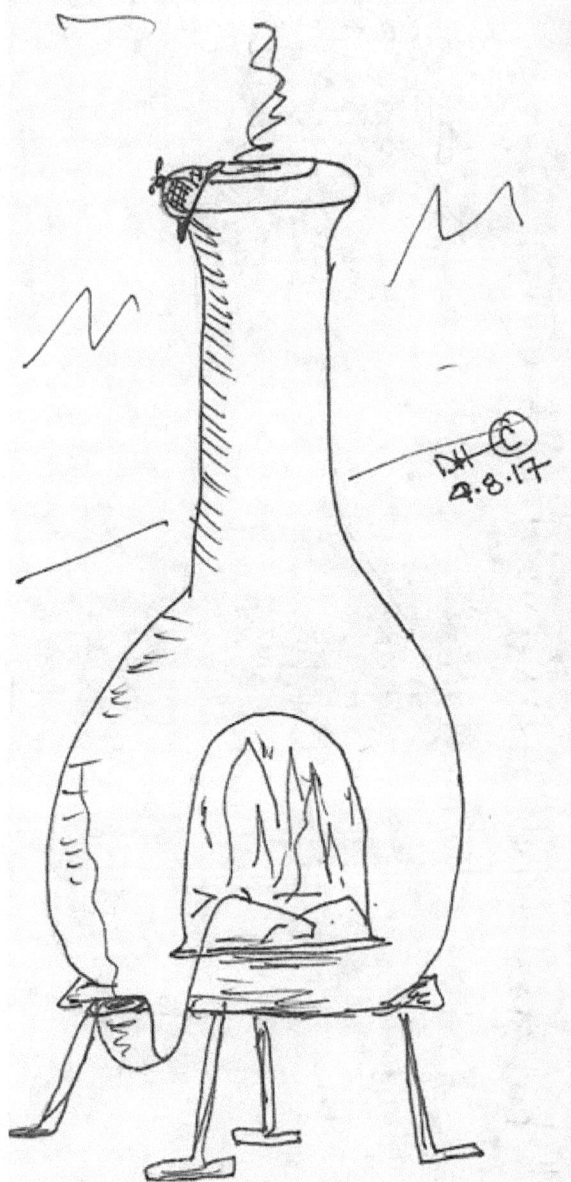

"...but the fire would naturally carry fumes
up the chimney..." DEVI

Sherlock Holmes
Is a Romo Fan

"...His little fan..." BRUC

Sherlock Holmes Inspects the Golden Gate Bridge

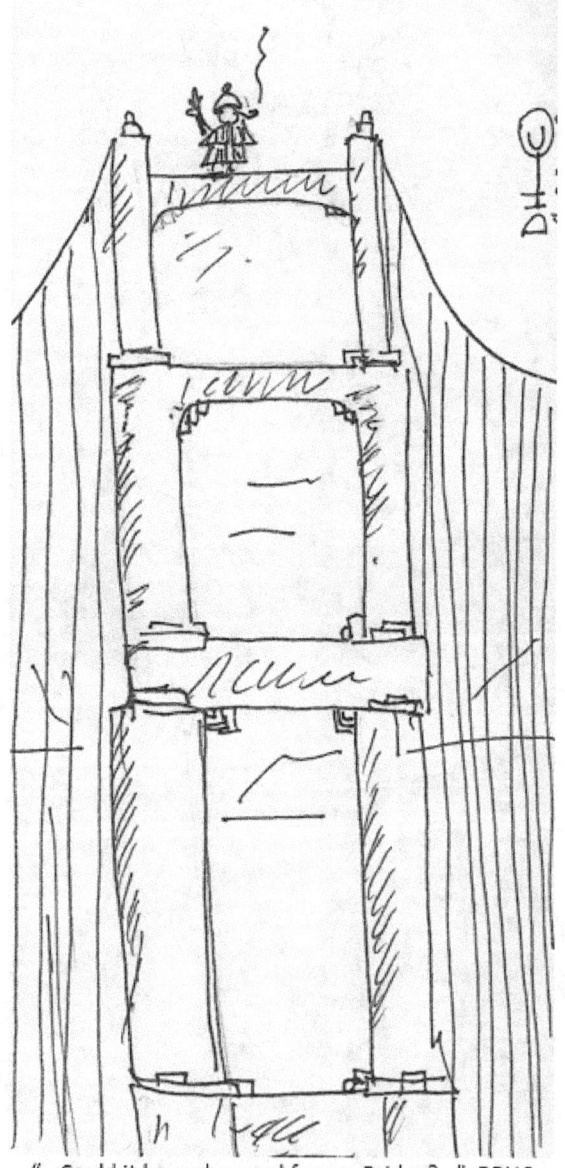

"...Could it have dropped from a Bridge?..." BRUC

Sherlock Holmes
Visits Suffolk, VA

"...Flourishing a cane as he walked. He swaggered..."
DANC

Sherlock Holmes
Taking It All In

"...I never thought of taking it seriously..." HOUN

Sherlock Holmes
Likes Piggly–Wiggly

"...It was a dreadful face – a Human pig..." VEIL

Sherlock Holmes
Admires the Phantom

"...Oh, you know the stories that the peasants tell about a phantom..." HOUN

Sherlock Holmes'
Moriarty Tatoo

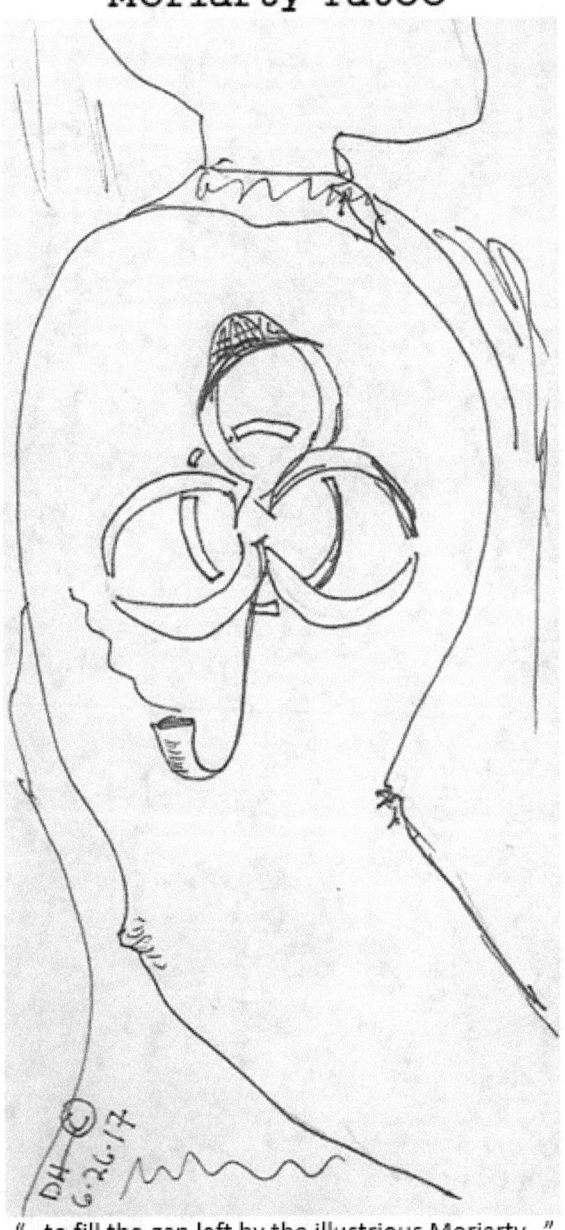

"...to fill the gap left by the illustrious Moriarty..."
MISS

Sherlock Holmes
Wine Stopper

"...He raised the cork and examined it minutely..." ABBE

Sherlock Holmes
At Wimbledon

"...beside the tennis lawn..." DANC

Sherlock Holmes
Incense

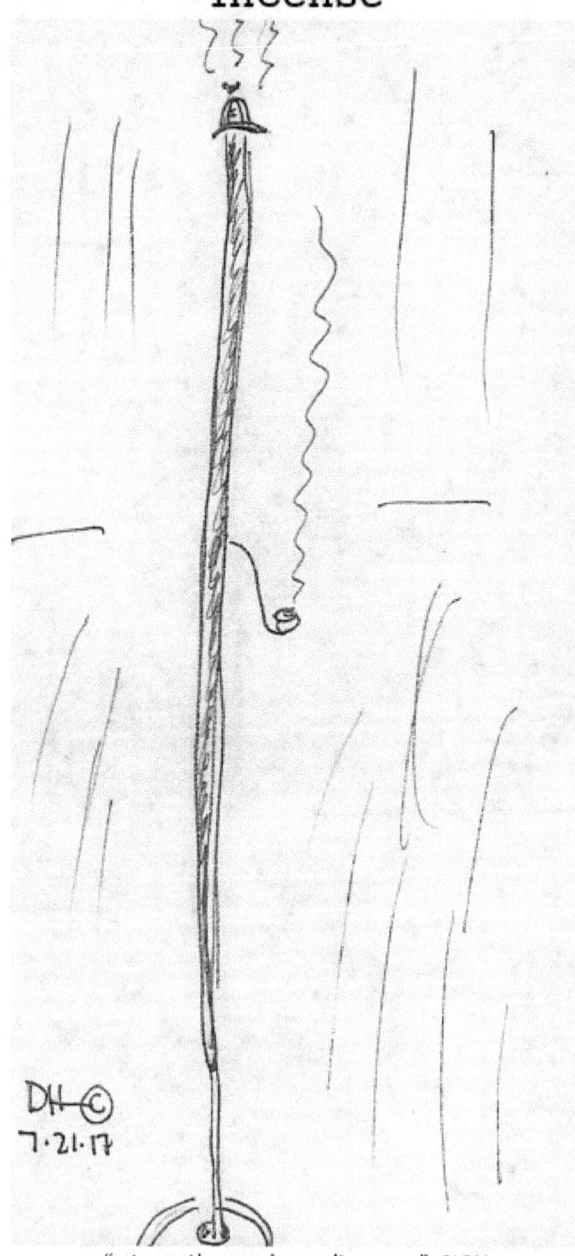

"...I saw the smoke curling up..." SIGN

Sherlock Holmes
A Clean Sweep

"...I took a wide sweep round..." PRIO

Sherlock Holmes
Has an Ice–Cream Cone

"...Theresa was cool as ice ..." ABBE

Sherlock Holmes
Inspects Gum Ally
San Luis Obispo, CA

"...I frequently found my thoughts turning in her direction and wondering what strange side-alley of a human experience this lovely-woman had strayed into..." COPP

Sherlock Holmes
Loves France

"...These pretended journys to France were rather cumbrous..." IDEN

Sherlock Holmes
Silly Walk

"...He is a big silly, bull-headed gungeon..."
MAZA

Sherlock Holmes the Napoleon of Crime Stoppers

"...No. No. No crime..." BLUE

Sherlock Holmes
Is a Good Habit

"...A member of the Roman Catholic Church..." CROO

Sherlock Holmes
Is Currently Popular

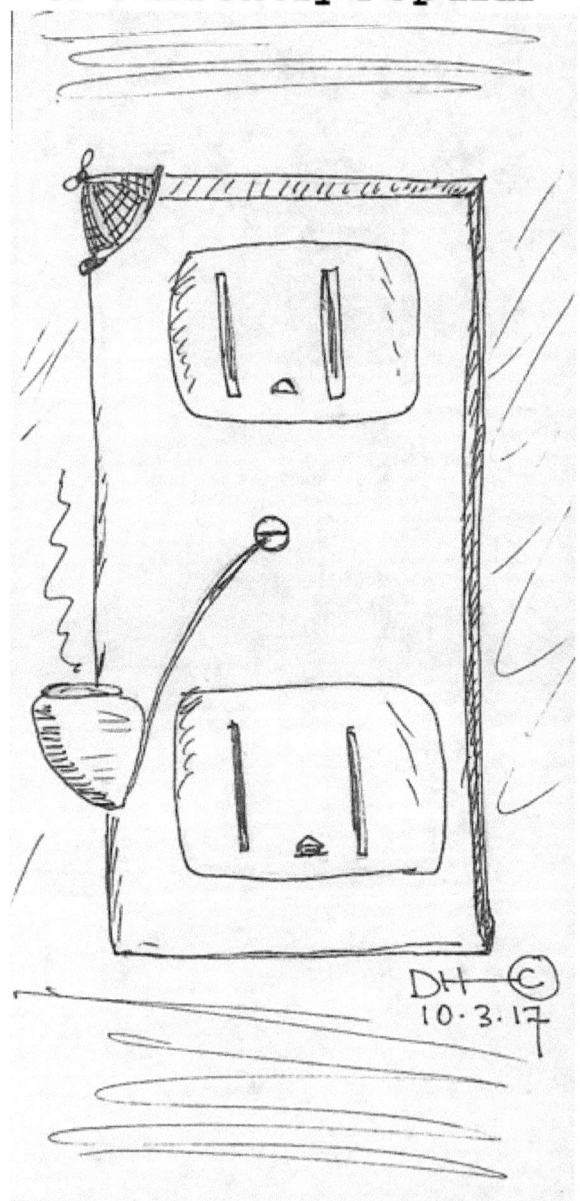

"...I wonder how a battery feels when it pours electricity into a non-conductor..." DYI N

Sherlock Holmes
Aims to Please

"...From the fanicful resenblence to the sound
produced by cocking a rifle..." FIVE

Sherlock Holmes
Enjoys KISS

"...Kiss it and make it well..." STUD

Sherlock Holmes
Respects the Flag

"...He kicked his heels together raised his hand in salute..." STUD

Sherlock Holmes
Sings Anchors Aweigh

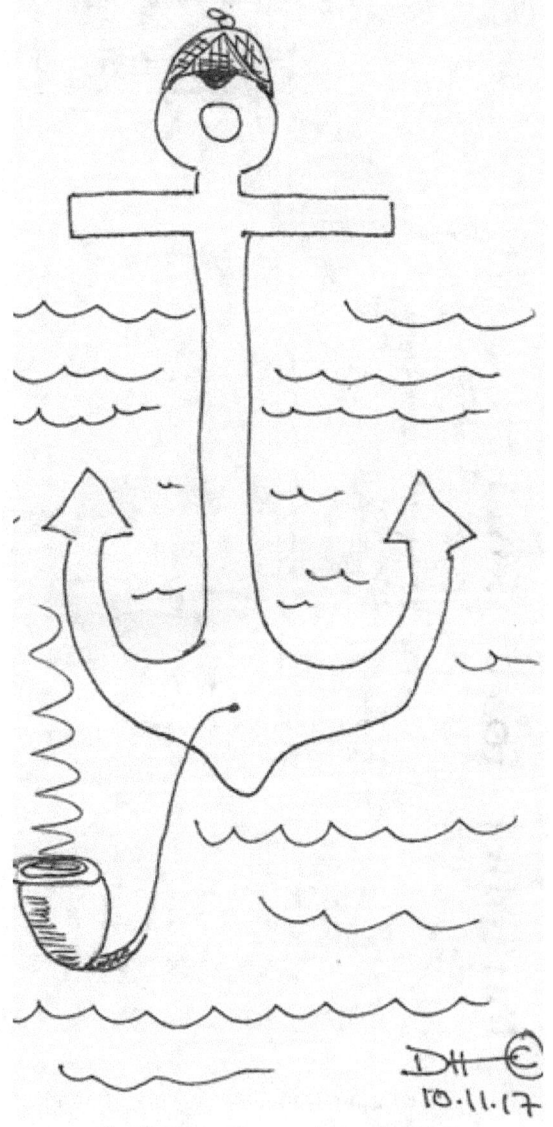

"...The dragging anchor..." DEVI

Sherlock Holmes Attends Texas–OU Weekend

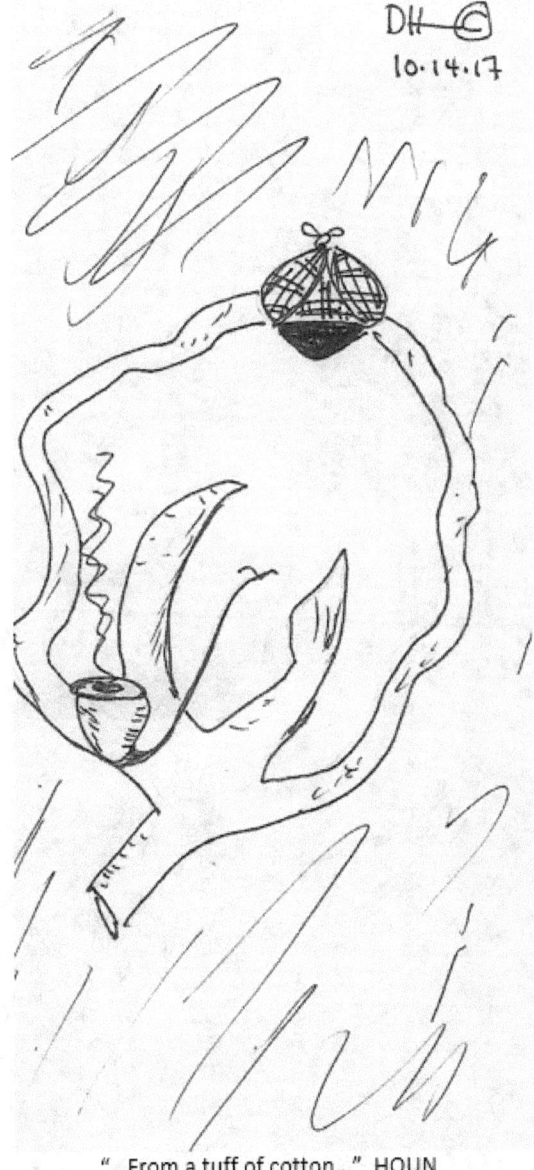

"...From a tuff of cotton..." HOUN

Sherlock Holmes
Indeed

"...The name was indeed well known to us..." BERY

Sherlock Holmes at The Precott, AZ Courthouse

"...I think we may take it that Prescott..." 3GAR

Sherlock Holmes
Stops on a Dime

"...If you only get a dime..." VALL

Sherlock Holmes
Graduates

"...I was at college..." GLOR

Sherlock Holmes Visits the Sequoia Redwood Forest

"...the most magnificent trees that I have ever seen..."
MUSG

Sherlock Holmes
Magnifying-Lolly

"...with his powerful magnifying lens..." BERY

Sherlock Holmes
Tops Everyone's Tree

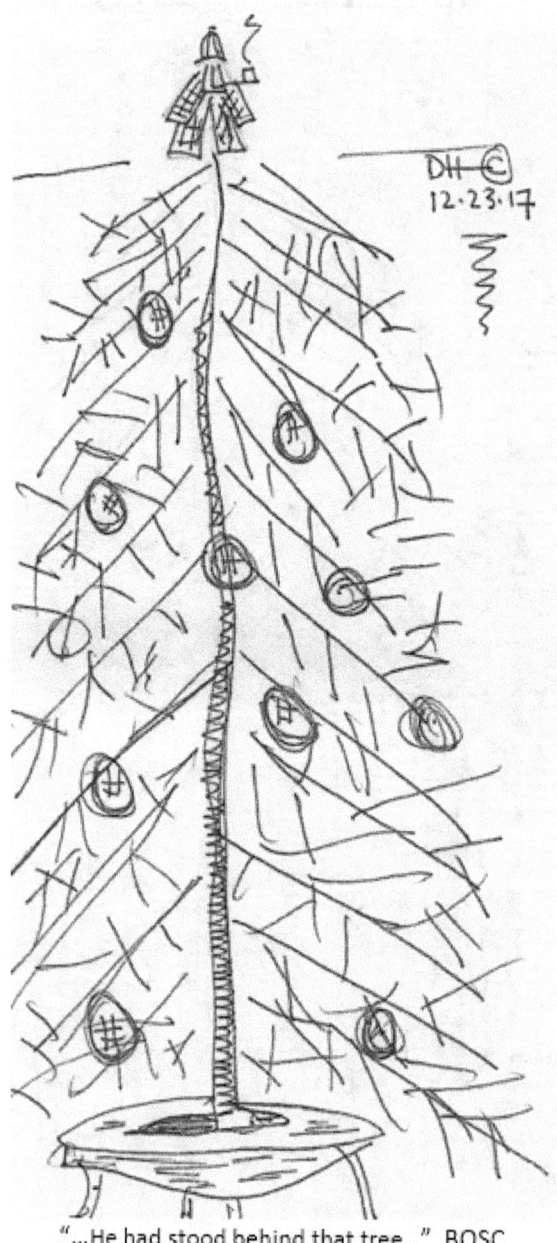

"...He had stood behind that tree..." BOSC

Sherlock Holmes:
Elf or Vulcan?

"...Where did he live then?..." IDEN

Sherlock Holmes:
First Down

"...you may find it pointing in an equally
uncompromising manner..." BSOC

Sherlock Holmes
On Boxing–Day

"...Bar fencing and boxing I had few atheletic tastes..."
GLOR

Sherlock Holmes
Visits Stanford

"...not only on the college but on the University..."
3STU

Sherlock Holmes
Returns to Egypt

"...Egypt..." LAST

Sherlock Holmes
Mourns the Dallas Cowboys

"...your client may rest in peace..." SCAN

Sherlock Holmes
Levitating

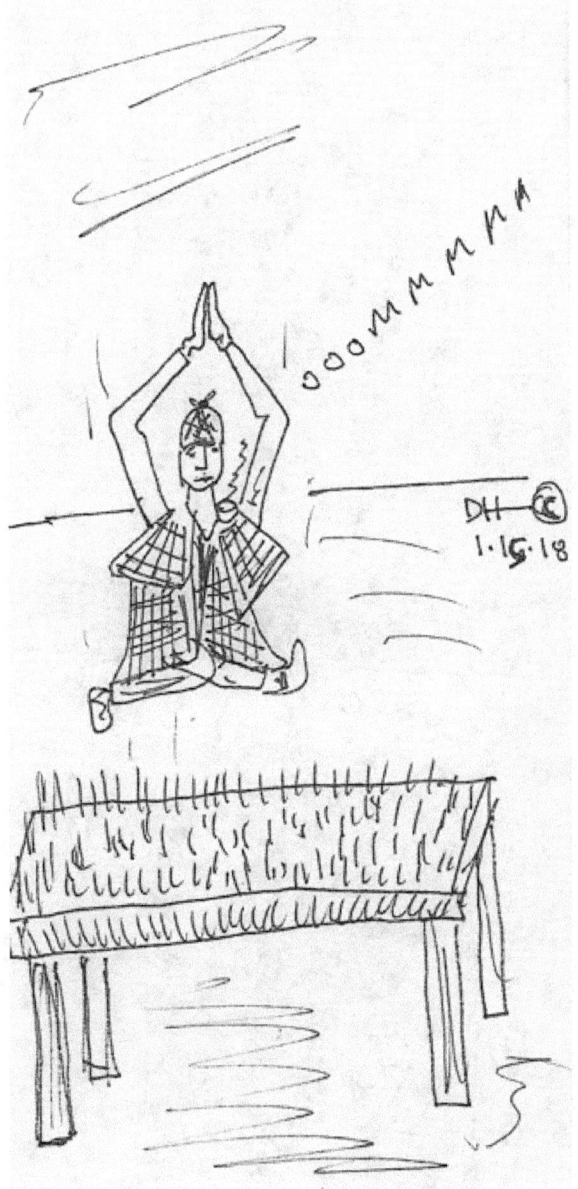

"...I have no doubt it was floating..." LION

Sherlock Holmes
Enters R.E.M.

"...for years I've been dreaming..." CROO

Sherlock Holmes
Gear—Head

"...Their winding gear may get out of order..."
VALL

Sherlock Holmes
Stomps Grapes

"...All of them tinged with wine   ..." ABBE

Sherlock Holmes
Dilly-Dilly

"...was nipped in the bud..." WIST

Sherlock Holmes
Overwhelmed with Data

"...data. Data, data, he cried..." COPP

Sherlock Holmes
Just Storking Around

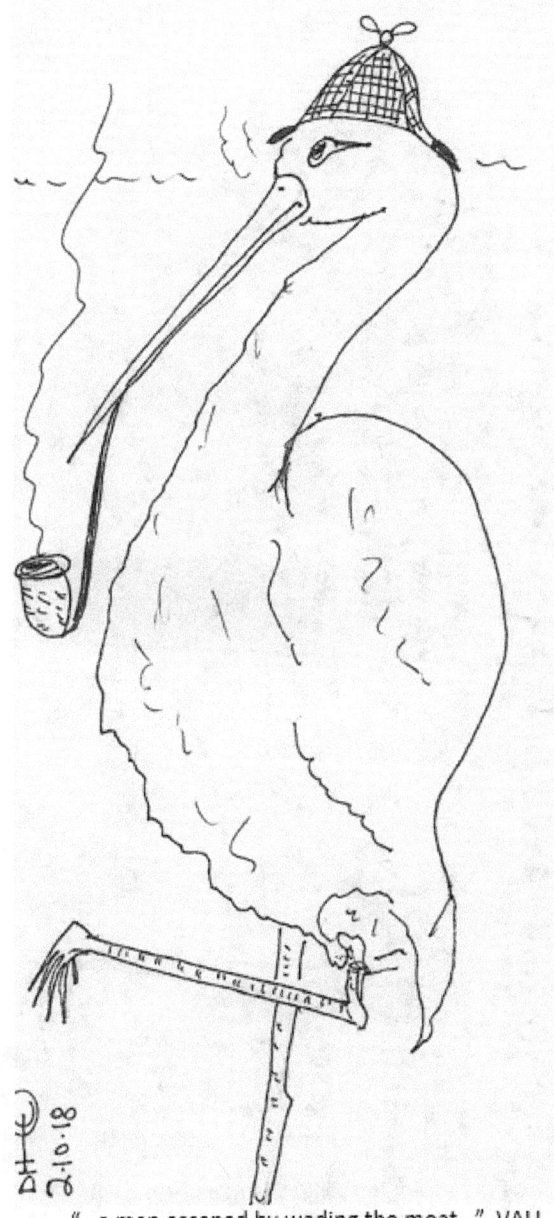

"...a man escaped by wading the moat..." VALL

Sherlock Holmes
With Sad Eyes

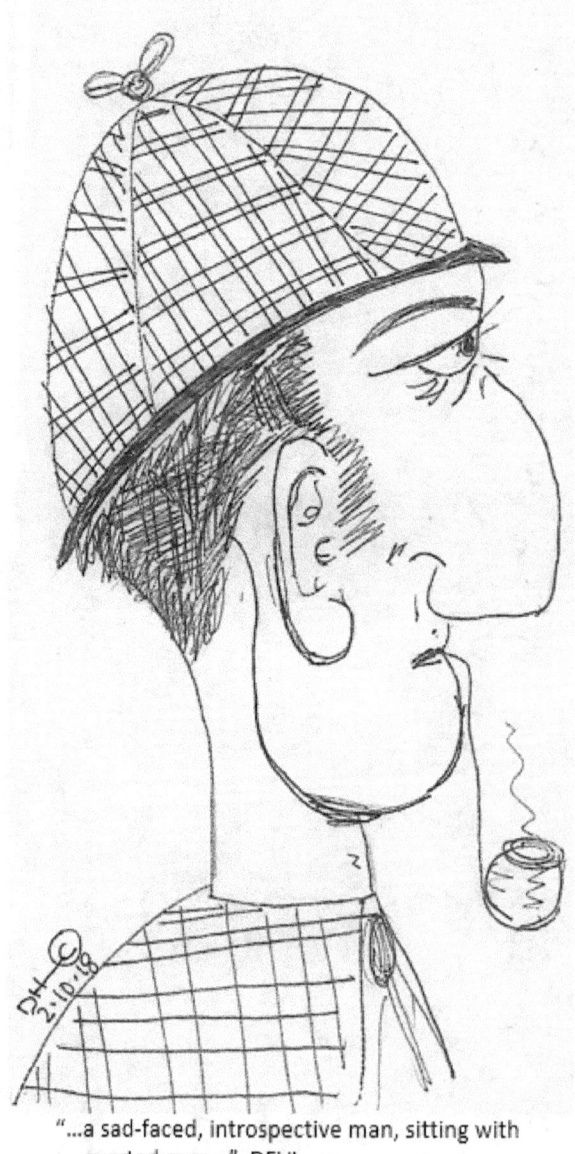

"...a sad-faced, introspective man, sitting with averted eyes..." DEVI

Sherlock Holmes:
The Nose Knows

"...with a thin, projecting nose..." EMPT

Sherlock Holmes:
Eyes Left

"...upon the left-hand side..." CROO

Sherlock Holmes
Enjoys a Bell-Pepper

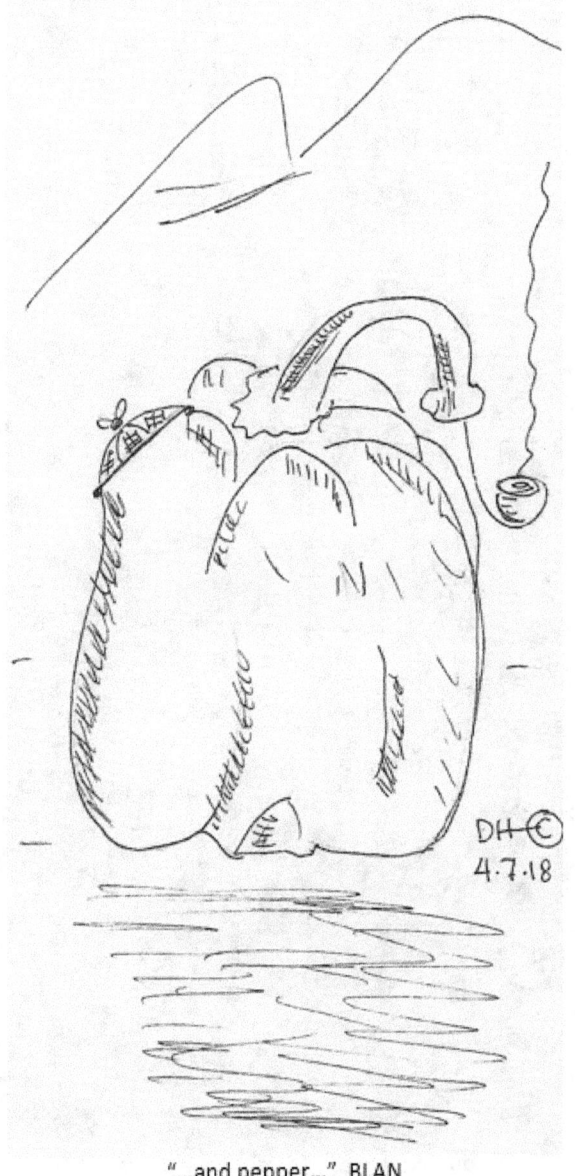

"...and pepper..." BLAN

Sherlock Holmes
Does the Fox-Trot

"...of country dances and of the meetings of fox hunters..." VALL

Sherlock Holmes
Paddle Boating

"...Stackhurst himself was a well-known rowing
Blue in his day..." LION

Sherlock Holmes Inflates His Dewlap

"...I distinctly saw his bare throat..." TWIS

Sherlock Holmes
Seen With 3–D

"...I thought you might be a little out of your depth..."
GREE

Sherlock Holmes
Loves the Pink Panther

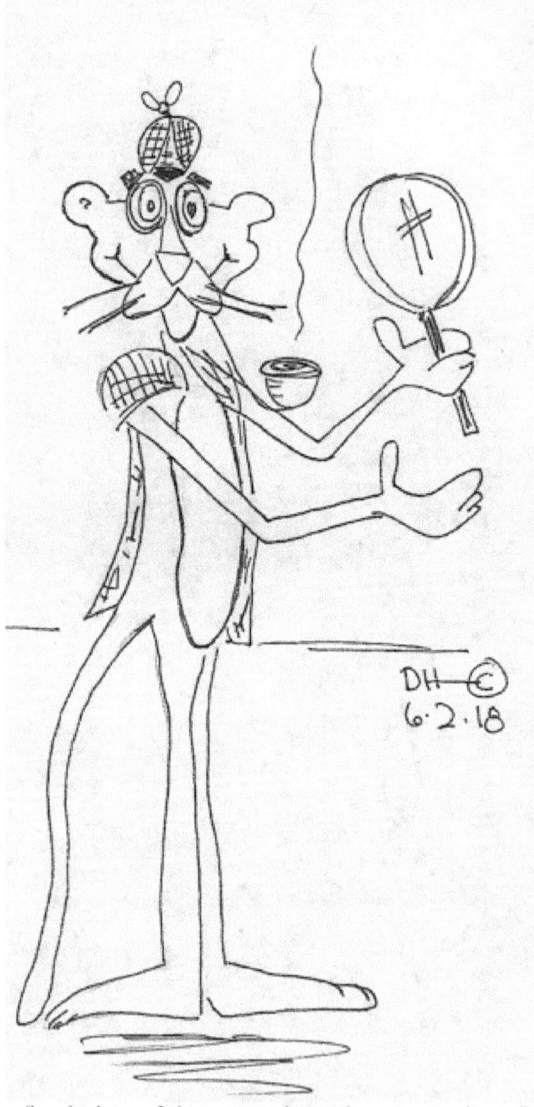

"...whiskers of that cut and a pink un protruding..."
BLUE

Sherlock Holmes
Admires the
Blue Angels

"...or the avenging angels..." STUD

Sherlock Holmes
Had No Father's Day
Wishes

"...It was quite against my wishes..." IDEN

Sherlock Holmes:
World Cup Fan

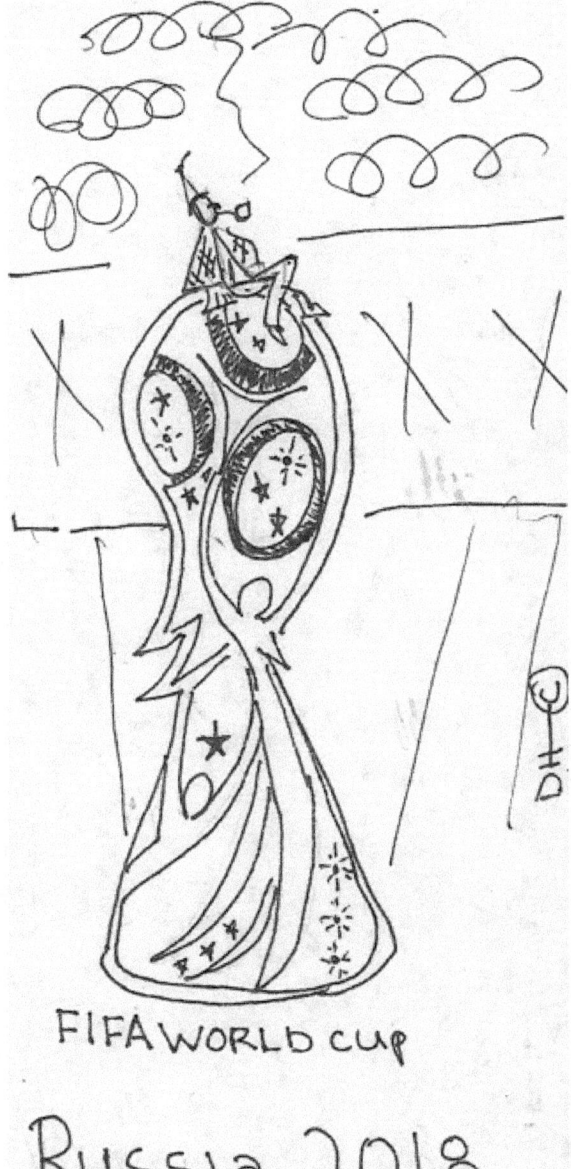

FIFA WORLD CUP

Russia 2018

"...What in the world can he have to do with it?..." BRUC

Sherlock Holmes
Just the Facts

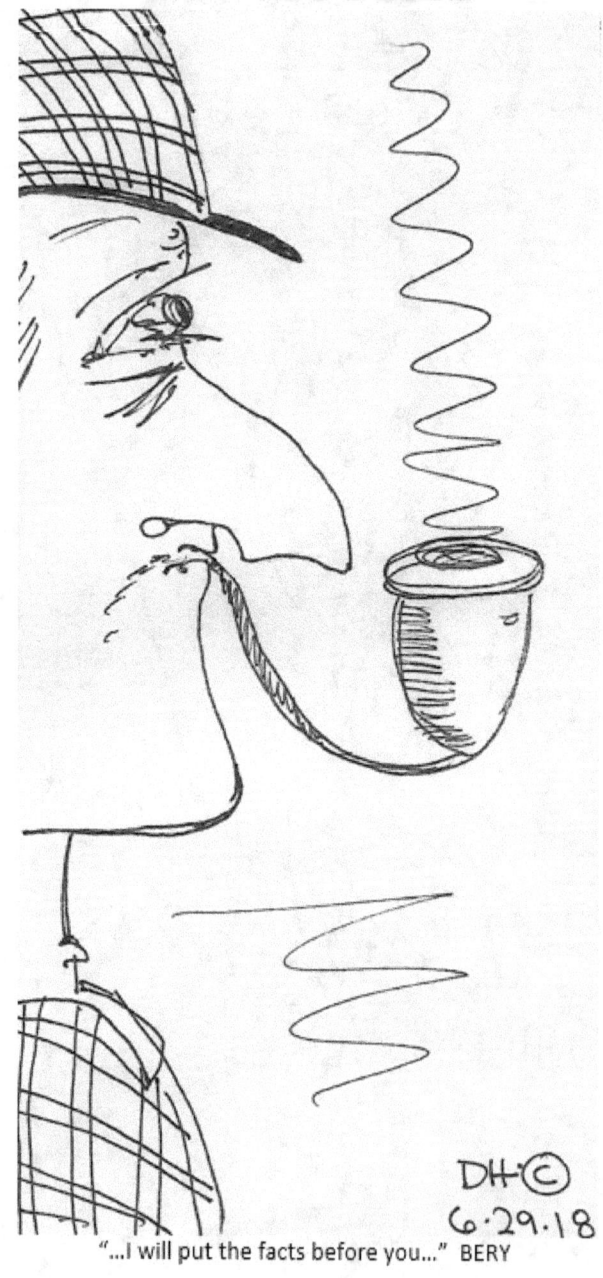

"...I will put the facts before you..." BERY

Sherlock Holmes
Tennis or Football?

"...I play the game for the game's own sake ..."
BRUC

Sherlock Holmes:
Via la France

"...Returning to France..." EMPT

Sherlock Holmes
Makes a Happy Buddha

"...He has been in China..." REDH

Sherlock Holmes
Can Smell a Liar

"...He knows already..." BERY

Sherlock Holmes
Not a Toga Fan

"...I am Greek by birth..." GREE

Sherlock Holmes
Sees What Other Miss

"...Where are the missing ones?..." BOSC

Sherlock Holmes
Loan Shark

"...Yes, and he's a shark..." MAZA

Sherlock Holmes:
Man for All Reasons

"...Your reasoning is certainly plausible..." BLUE

Holmes Sweet Home

"...Apply 221B Baker Street..." NAVA

Sherlock Holmes:
Chanelling Mycroft

DH©
7·31·18

"...Making the rest of him seem the more obese and
unnatural by contrast..." RESI

Sherlock Holmes
Visits Yosemite

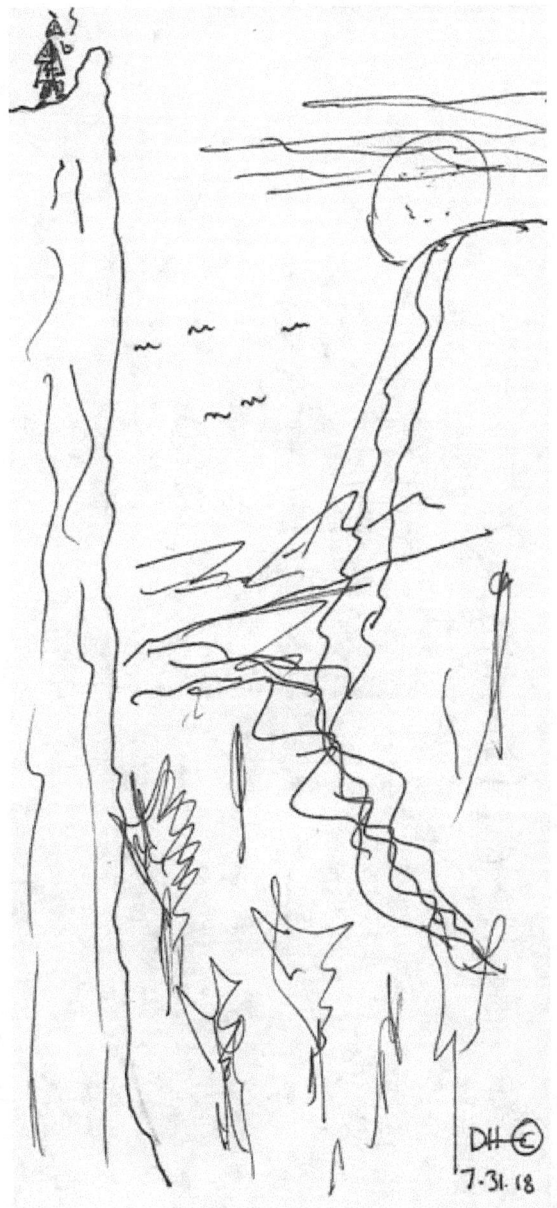

"...From Califoria..." NOBL

Sherlock Holmes
Ain't No Robot

"...You really are an automaton..." SIGN

Sherlock Holmes Enjoys Jacques Pepin's Chicken

".She's a stray chicken..." LADY

Sherlock Holmes
Always There

DH ©
8.14.18

"...But always there was something new..." CREE

Sherlock Holmes Uses Stairs in Case of Fire

"...He was morbidly nervous of fire, and always kept his beside him, so that he might escape..." RESI

Sherlock Holmes
Remembers 9.11.2001

"...I have said that scattered towers..." DEVI

Sherlock Holmes
Loves King-Kong

"...and idlers of the Empire..." STUD

Sherlock Holmes
Enjoys Old Radio Plays

DH–G
9·16·68

"...It was my old housekeeper who heard of it first
by the strange wireless..." LION

Sherlock Holmes:
A Real Teddy Bear

"...Bear in mind..." HOUN

Sherlock Holmes
Amid Morning Glories

"...told of the glory..." DANC

Sherlock Holmes
Inspects the Harvest

"...yet we add more sheaf to our harvest..." BRUC

Sherlock Holmes
Loves the N.H.L.

"...In the states and in Canada..." HOUN

Sherlock Holmes
Great Mascot.

"...Cheer up, Watson..." DEVI

Sherlock Holmes
Great View

"...commanding a great view..." NAVA

Sherlock Holmes
Visits Coney Island

"...At the nature of the child's amusement..." COPP

Sherlock Holmes
Would Vote if He Could

"...when next it comes to a vote..." VALL

Sherlock Holmes
Does Glue

"...It is glue, Watson..." SHOS

Sherlock Holmes
Visits Gotham City

"...see what his object was in this stealthy nocturnal
visit..." BLAC

Sherlock Holmes
Nail–Biter

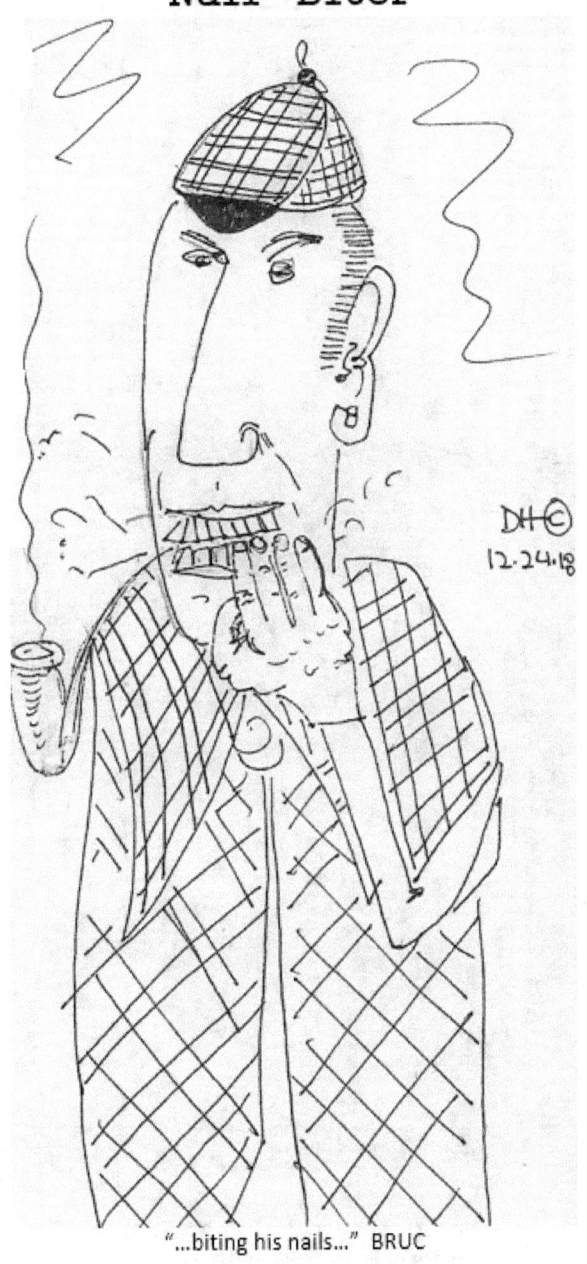

"...biting his nails..." BRUC

Sherlock Holmes
Loves Times Square

"...He passed the grounds and looked at the square of light..." BRUC

Sherlock Holmes
Tree Hugger

"...I sat up half the night hugging myself over it..." STOC

Sherlock Holmes
Points the Way

"...I see the direction in which all things point..." BOSC

Sherlock Holmes
Mer–Man

"...Neither Dog, not cat, nor monkey nor any creature
that we are familiar with..." CREE

Sherlock Holmes
With a Twisted Lip

"...The twisted lip which had given the repulsive sneer to the face..." TWIS

Sherlock Holmes
Infiltrates the K.K.K.

"...have you never," said Sherlock Holmes bending
forward and sinking his voice, "have you never
heard of the Ku Klux Klan?..." FIVE

Sherlock Holmes
Ain't No Blue Meanie

"...save that it is blue in shade..." BLUE

Sherlock Holmes
Likes Groot

"...But what is the root of it?..." REDC

Sherlock Holmes
Likes College Hoops

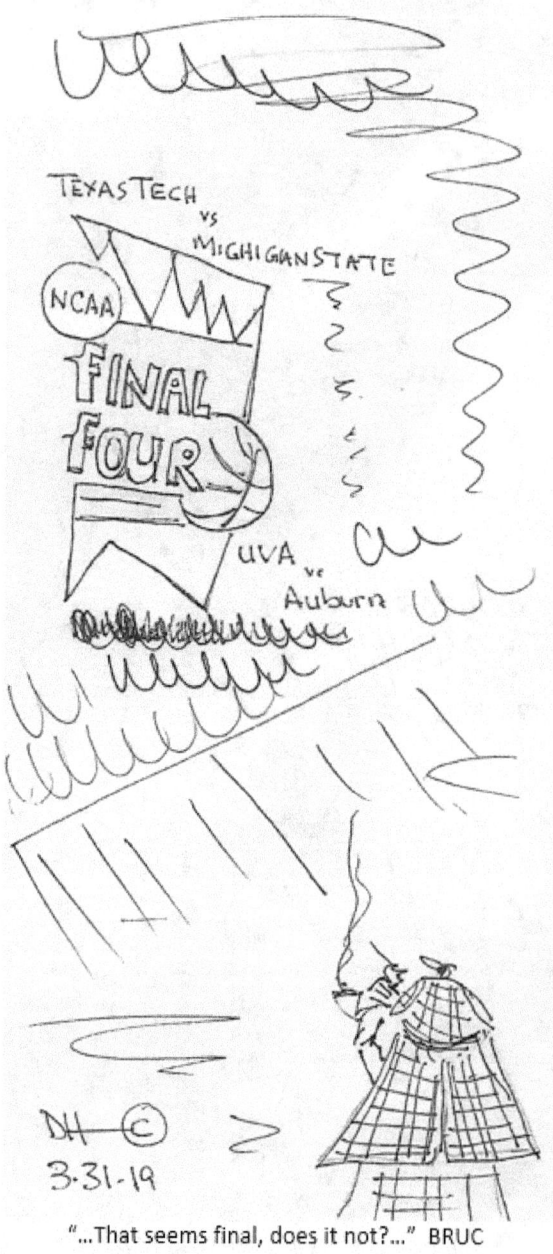

TEXAS TECH vs MICHIGAN STATE

NCAA FINAL FOUR

UVA vs Auburn

DH © 3·31·19

"...That seems final, does it not?..." BRUC

Sherlock Holmes
Is Such a Hoe

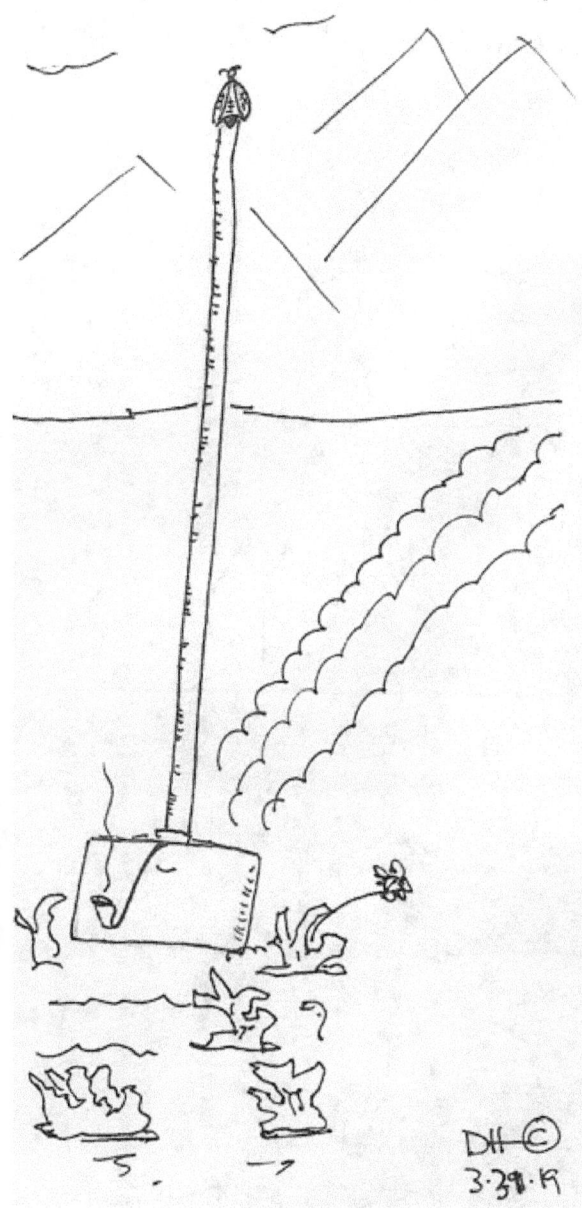

"...Knows nothing of practicle gardening..." STUD

Sherlock Holmes
Respects Dirk Nowitzki

"...His name is Vicent Spaulding..." REDH

Sherlock Holmes
Dreams of William Tell

"...Fitting a flint-tipped arrow on to the string of his bow...." HOUN

Sherlock Holmes
Poses for
Touloose–Lautrec

DH ©
4·28·19

"...I traced him back to Paris..." WIST

Sherlock Holmes Likes Old School Hockey

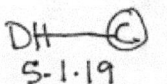

DH —C
5-1-19

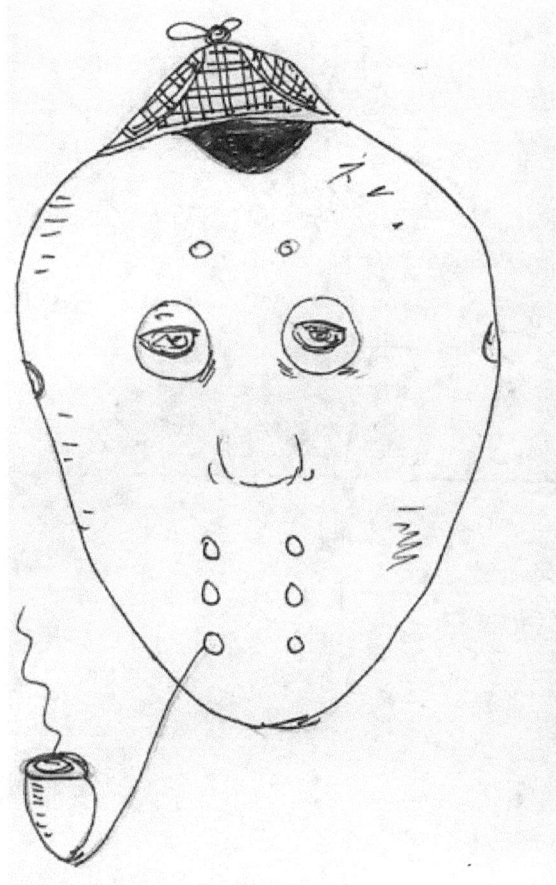

"...Excellent! And a mask?..." CHAS

127

Sherlock Holmes
Still Cycling Solitary

"...I am told he is an excellent cyclist..." PRIO

Sherlock Holmes:
Happy Cinco de Mayo

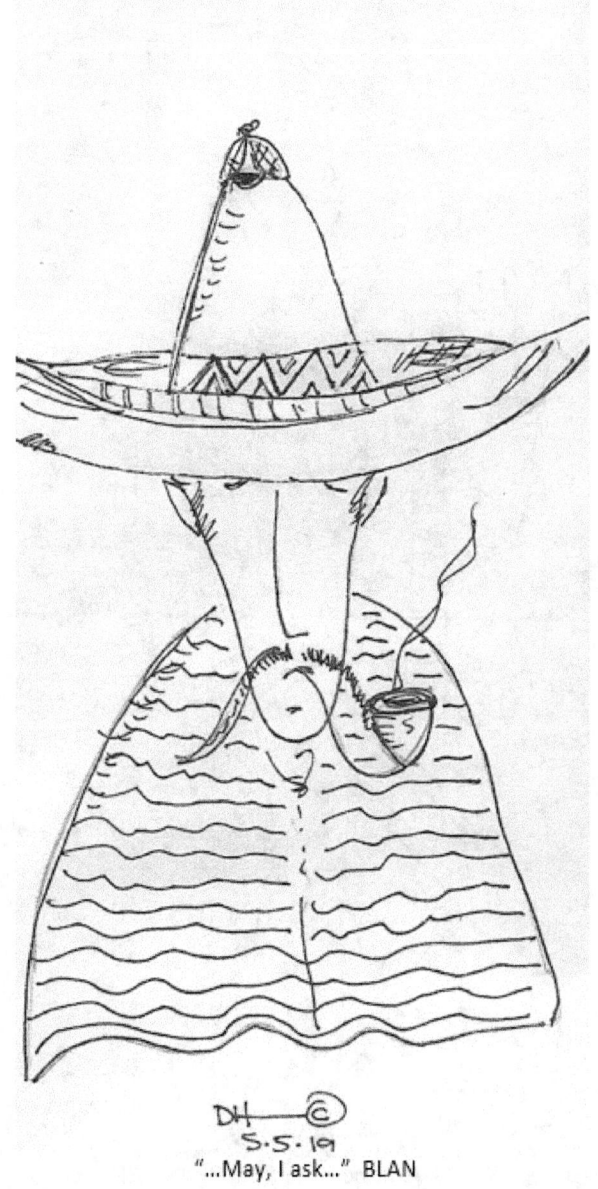

DH ©
5.5.19
"...May, I ask..." BLAN

Sherlock Holmes
Swears to No One

"...He sweras he knew nothing..." SIGN

Sherlock Holmes
King of the Hives

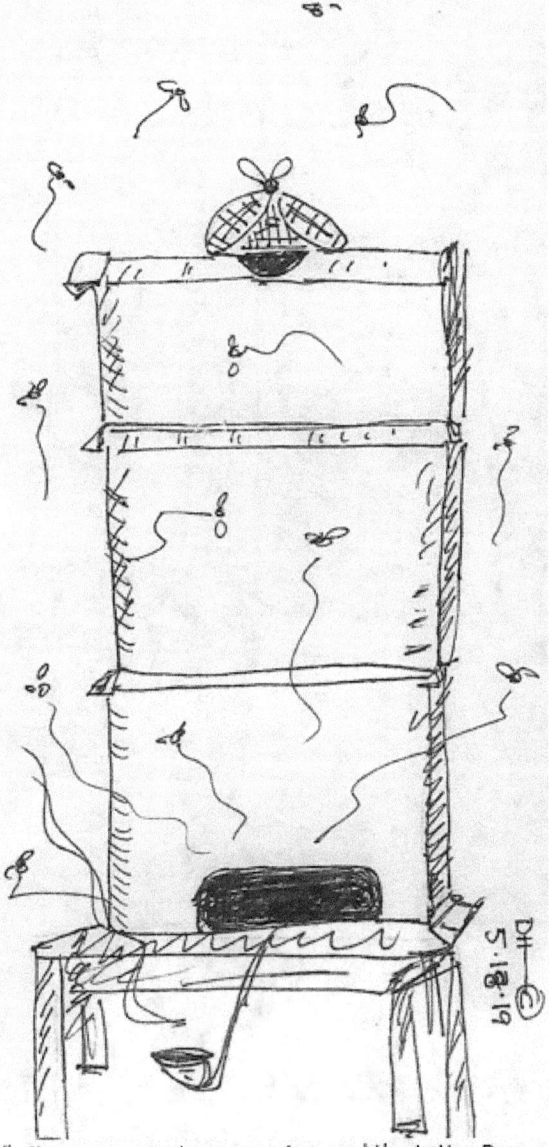

"...It was a warm June morning, and the Latter Day
Saints were busy as the bees whose hive they have
chosen for the emblem..." STUD

Sherlock Holmes
Heats-Up

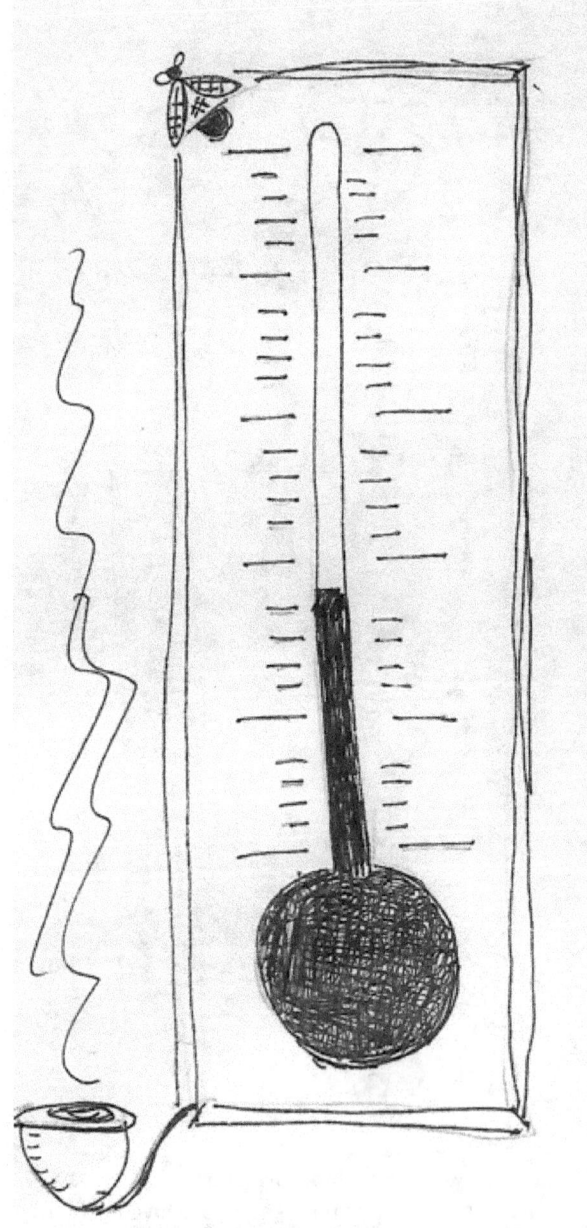

"...involved much heating of retorts..." SIGN

Sherlock Holmes
Is Into Orchids

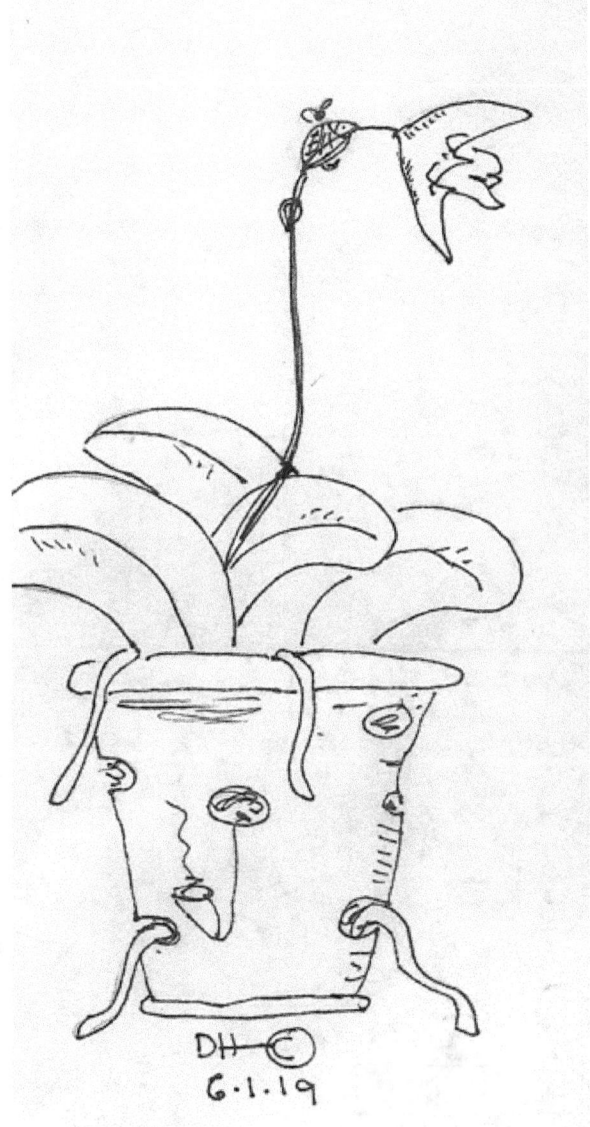

"...we are very rich with orchids on the moors..." HOUN

Sherlock Holmes
Climbs Mt. Everest

elev. 29,029'

DH ©
6.5.19

"...On the extreme verge of the horizon lies a long chain of mountains..." STUD

Sherlock Holmes
Remembers D–Day

"...He went off to France..." IDEN

Sherlock Holmes:
What? Me Worry?

"...I'd only ask you not to worry..." VALL

Sherlock Holmes
Melts in the Texas Heat

DH ©
8·13·19

"...Can you rise superior to the heat..." CARD

Sherlock Holmes
Good-Luck Dragonfly

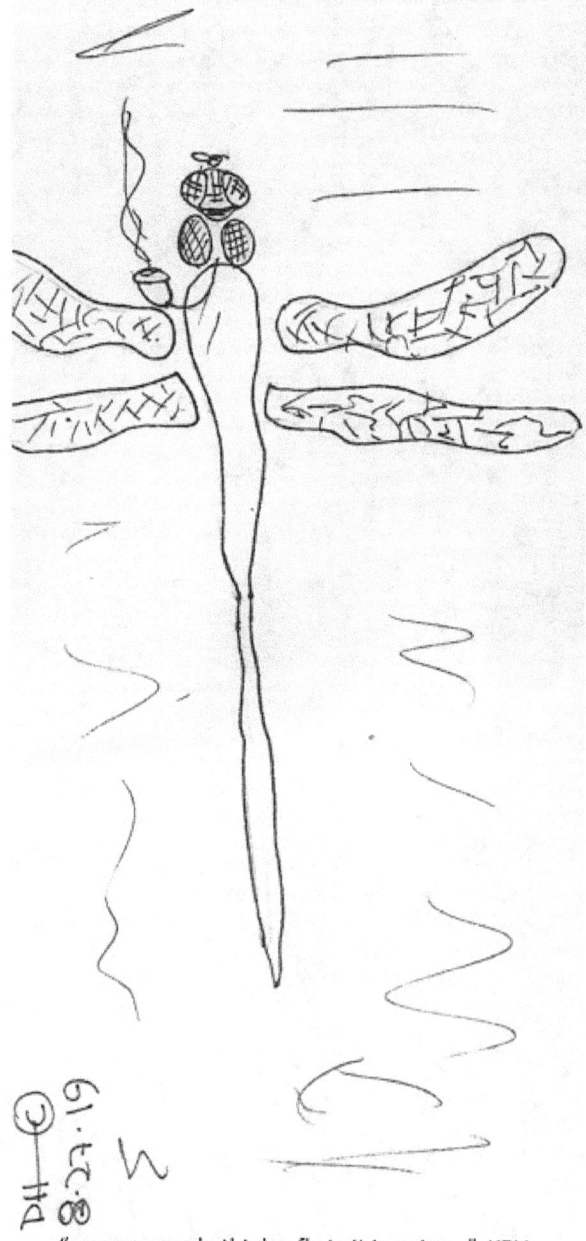

"...some people think a fly in it is a sign..." YELL

Sherlock Holmes
Reads Dr. Seuss

"...when I realized that it was a cat..." CHAS

Sherlock Holmes
Composting

"...and beds of decaying vegetation..." SIGN

Sherlock Holmes'
Corona Virus Protection

"...your protection, Sahib..." SIGN

Sherlock Holmes
Has Peas of Mind

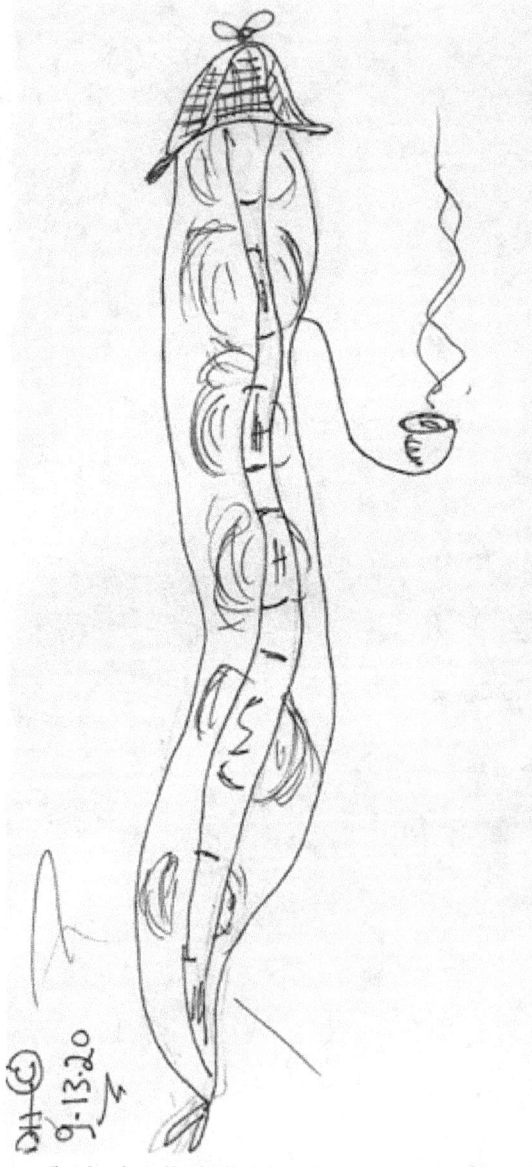

"...the landlady babbled of green peas at
seven-thirty..."   3STU

DH ©
9·19·20

"...all four..." REDC

Sherlock Holmes
Thinks Some Teams Suck

"...a driver shouted at his team..." STUD

Sherlock Holmes
Looks Long and Hard

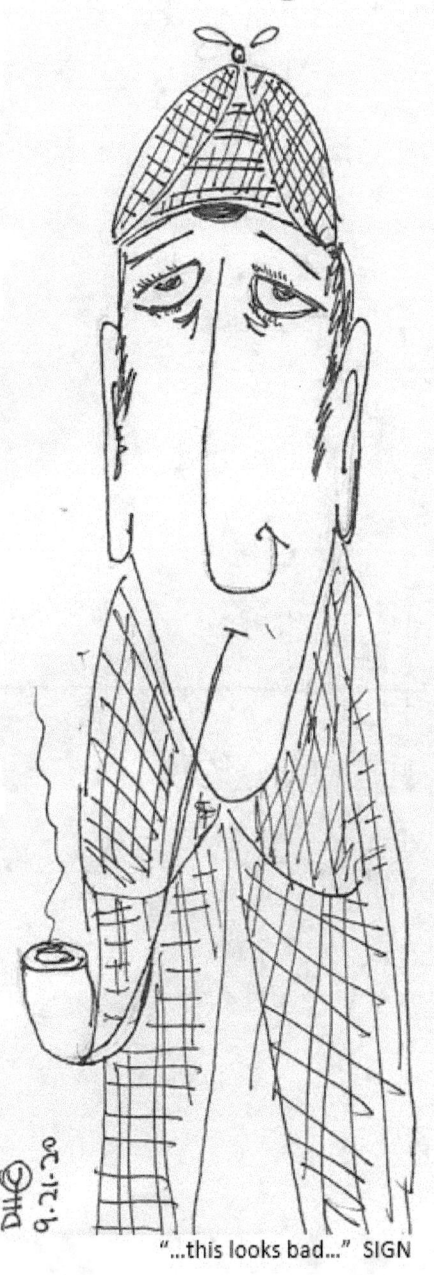

"...this looks bad..." SIGN

Sherlock Holmes'
Big Haul

DH €)
10·7·2020

"...we were able to haul him out..." SIGN

Sherlock Holmes
Billy the Page

"...I saw an ill-dressed vagabond in the lane
yesterday evening..." BERY

Sherlock Holmes
Displays His Beatles'
Haircut

"...with a shock of raven hair which fell to his collar..." |
VALL

Sherlock Holmes: The Devil Made Him Do It

"...I believe you are the devil himself..." MAZA

Sherlock Holmes In Elizabethan I Era

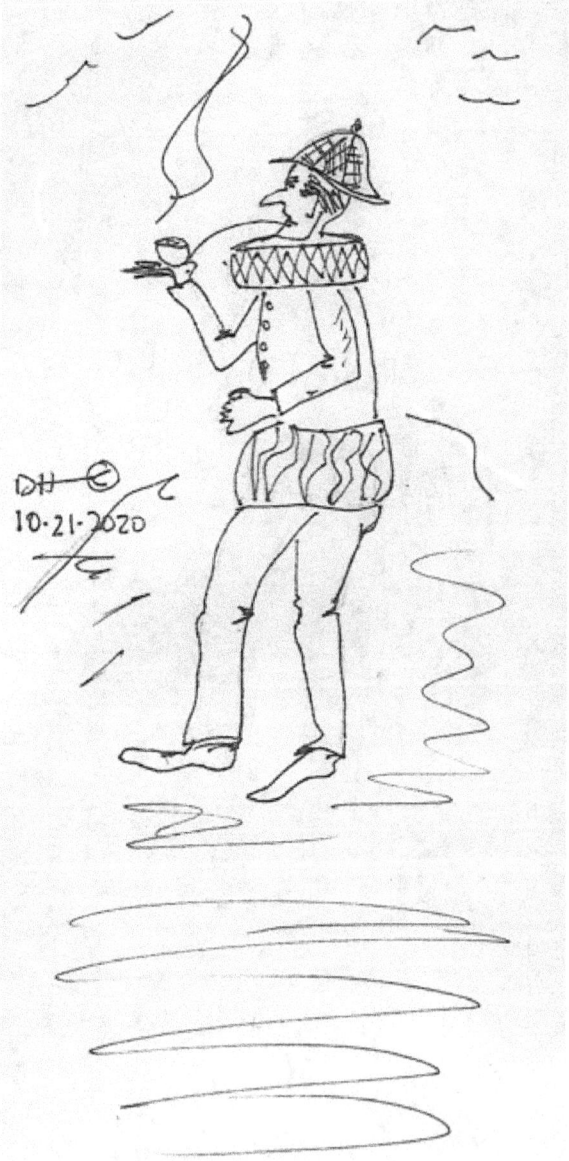

"...in every variety of dress, from the Elizabethan knight..." HOUN

Sherlock Holmes
Hatchet Thrower

"...for one of those, I picked up a battle-axe..." MUSG

Sherlock Holmes
Life of the Party

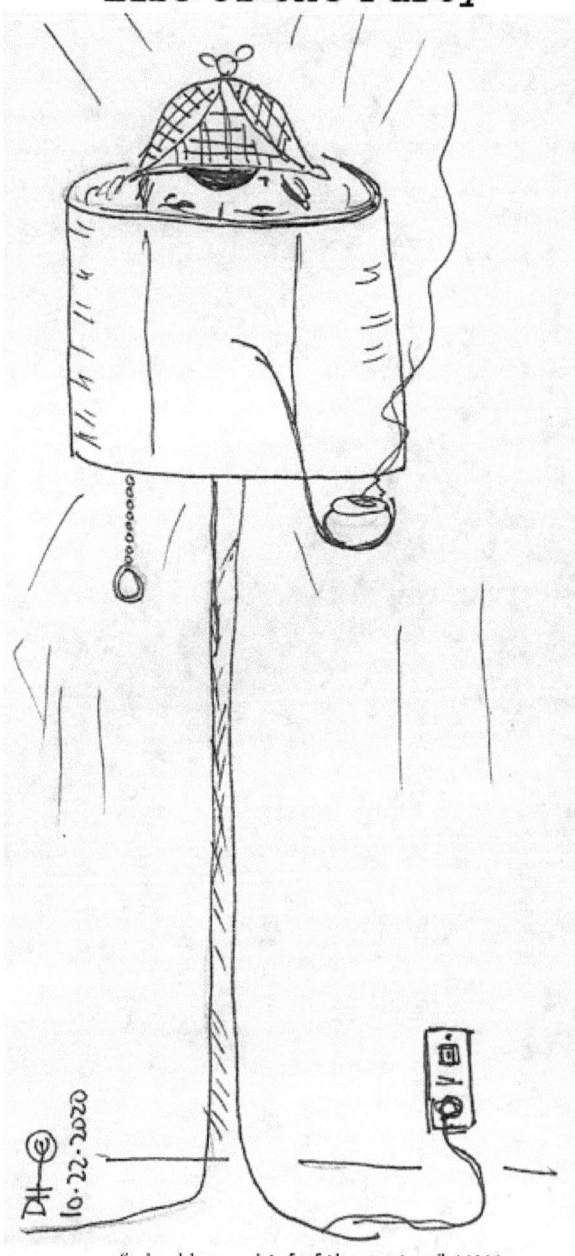

"...had been chief of the party..." VALL

Sherlock Holmes'
Feelings of the Pandemic

"...we were all three dumbfounded..." STUD

Sherlock Holmes
Judges Gymnastics

"...well, we cannot expect to score every time..." NAVA

Sherlock Holmes
Headphones

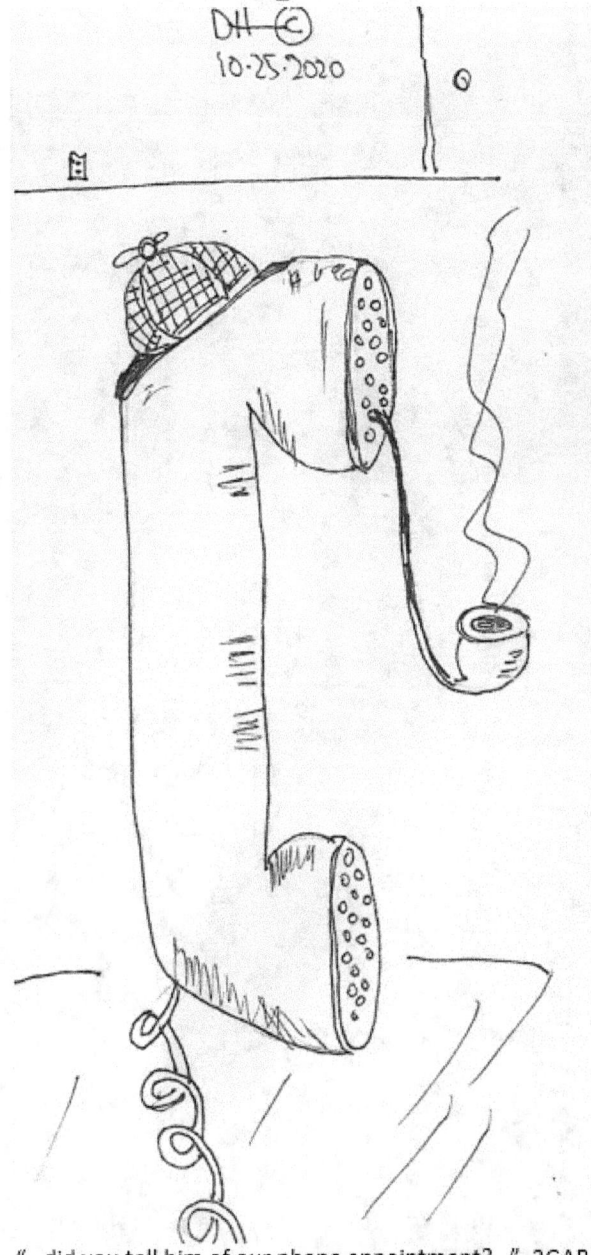

"...did you tell him of our phone appointment?..." 3GAB

Sherlock Holmes
The Friendly Ghost

"…There was, to my mind, something eerie and
ghost-like…" SIGN

Sherlock Holmes:
Afrin– A 7% Solution

"...Well, there seems to me to be only one possible solution..."   COPP

Sherlock Holmes
Loves What-a-Burger

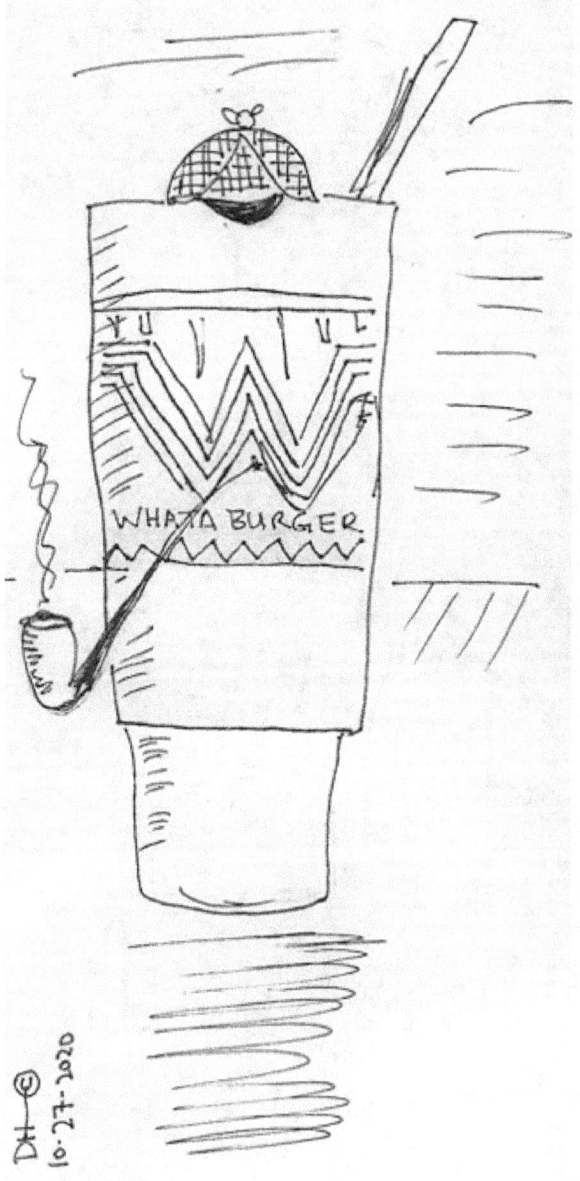

"...a little good Berkshire beef would do him no harm..."
ENGI

Sherlock Holmes
Will Miss Alex Trebek

"...a man might play a deep game..." REDH

Sherlock Holmes
Grand Master

DH ©
8·10·2020

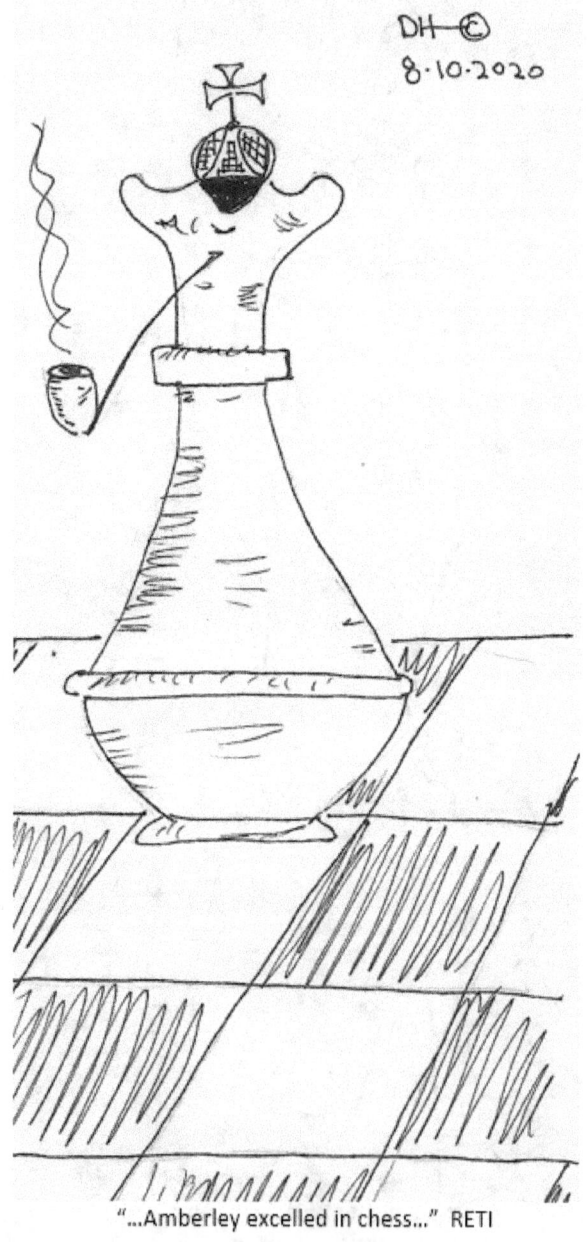

"...Amberley excelled in chess..." RETI

Sherlock Holmes
Translates Fine

"...to make an easy and common transition..." NOBL

Sherlock Holmes
Flower Child

"…I strove to keep peace…" GLOR

Sherlock Holmes Congratulates the New President

"...I trust I shall soon have to congratulate you..." ABBE

Sherlock Holmes Knows the Meaning of Life

"...what the true meaning of it can be..." BRUC

Sherlock Holmes
Likes His iPhone 12

"...there must be a communication..." SPEC

Sherlock Holmes
Reads Edgar Allen Poe

"...but he was by no means such a phenomenon as Poe
appeared to imagine..."   STUD

Sherlock Holmes
Makes another 1st Down

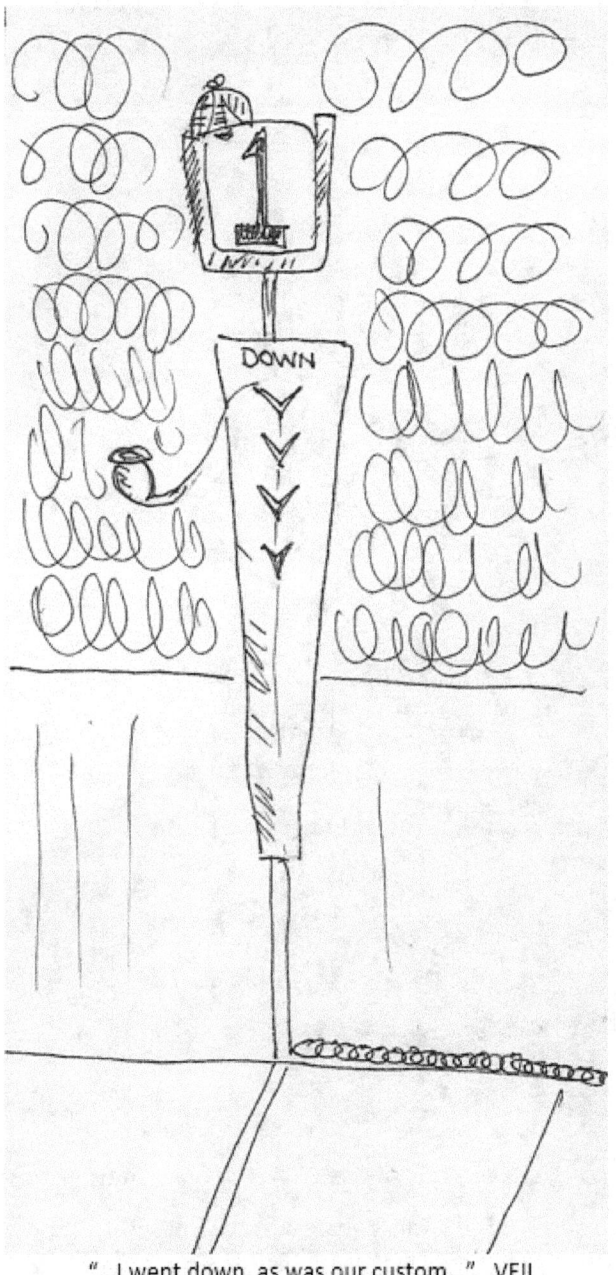

"...I went down, as was our custom..."   VEIL

Sherlock Holmes Found Zero Election Fraud

"...the whole affair must be some great hoax or fraud..."   REDH

Sherlock Holmes
Has a Question, Mark

"...What's this mark?..." VALL

Sherlock Holmes Could Have Been a Beetle

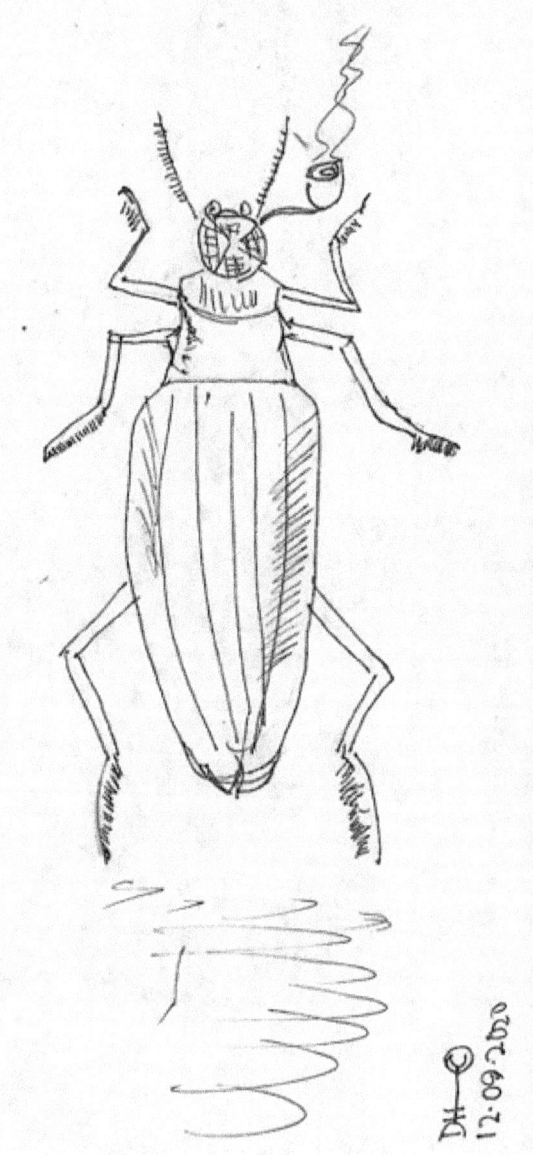

"...he was pinned like a beetle to a card..." BLAC

Sherlock Holmes
Believes in Vaccinations

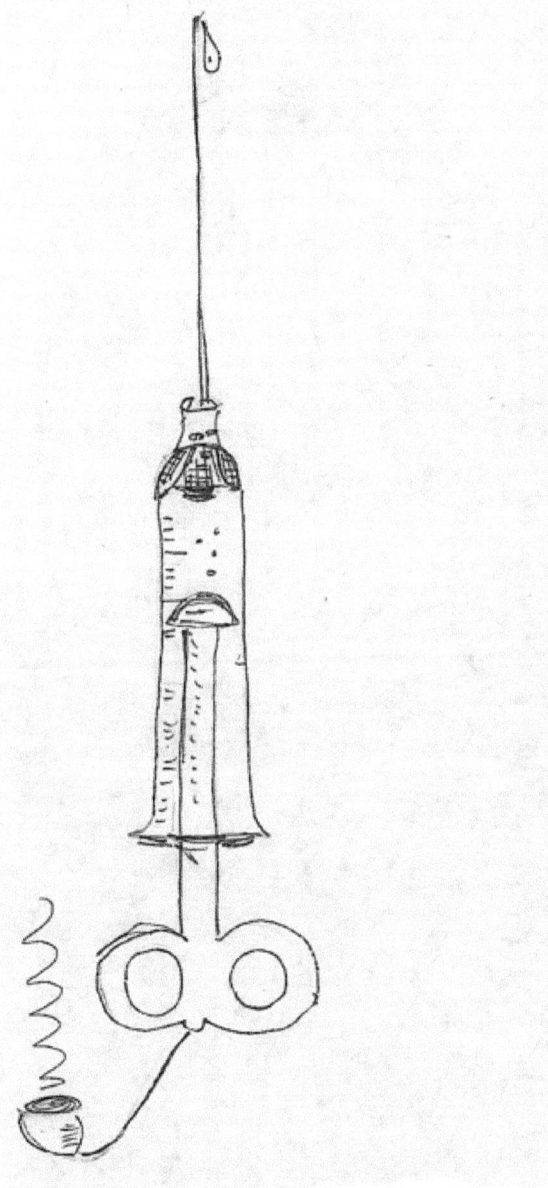

"...he adjusted the delicate needle..." SIGN

Sherlock Holmes
Believes in Masks

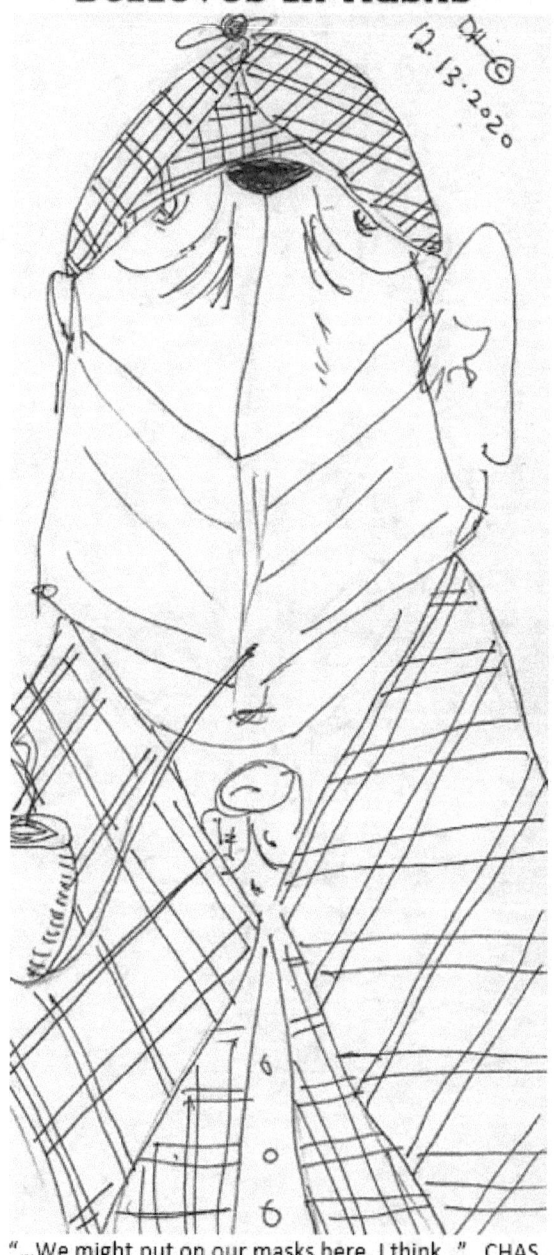

"...We might put on our masks here, I think..."   CHAS

Sherlock Holmes'
Charlie Brown
Christmas Tree

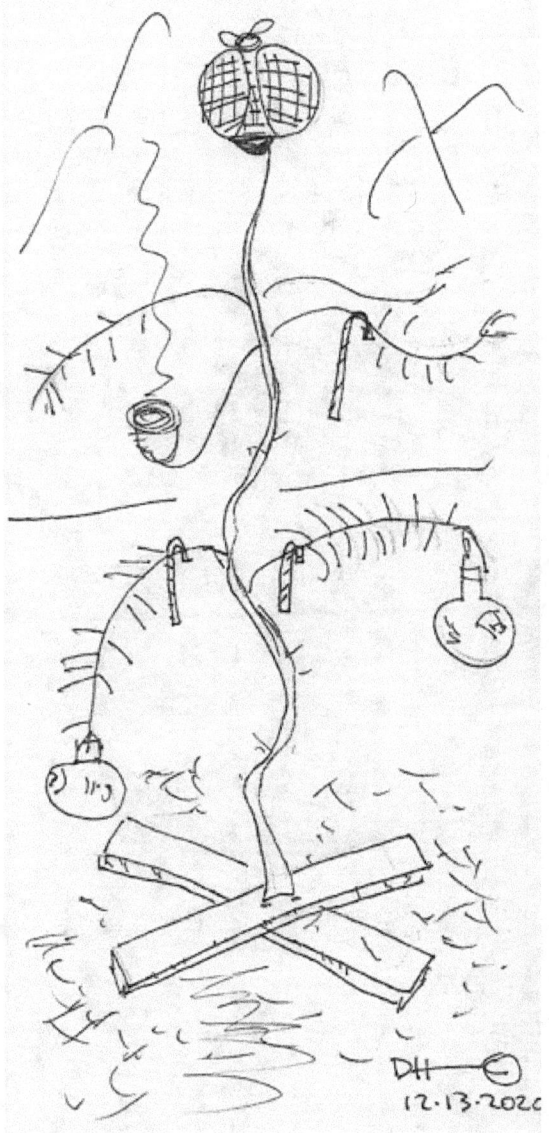

"...upon the second morning after Christmas..."   BLUE

Sherlock Holmes
Nutcracker

"...He was a young man with a clear, hairless
face, a long nose, and rather nutcracker
jaws..." GLOR

Sherlock Holmes
On a Shelf

"...you could just fill that gap on the second shelf..."   EMPT

Sherlock Holmes Contemplates Life

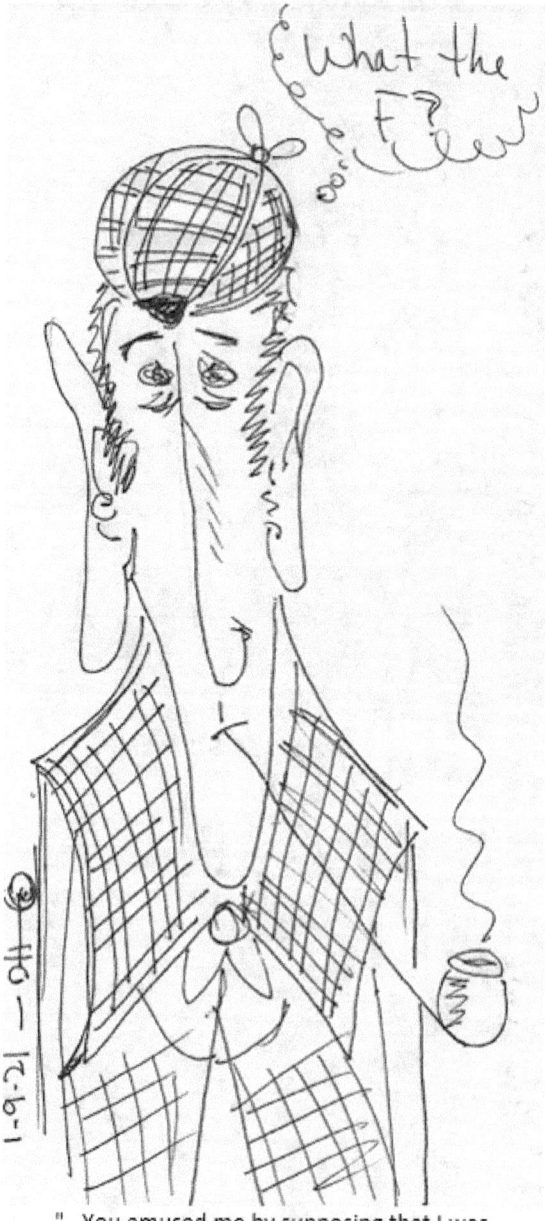

"...You amused me by supposing that I was contemplating the possibility..." 3STU

Sherlock Holmes
High-Heel Sneakers

"...and an unlaced pair of canvas shoes..." LION

Sherlock Holmes In a
Reflective Mood

"...I have just been thinking..."   SIGN

Sherlock Holmes:
Never a Question

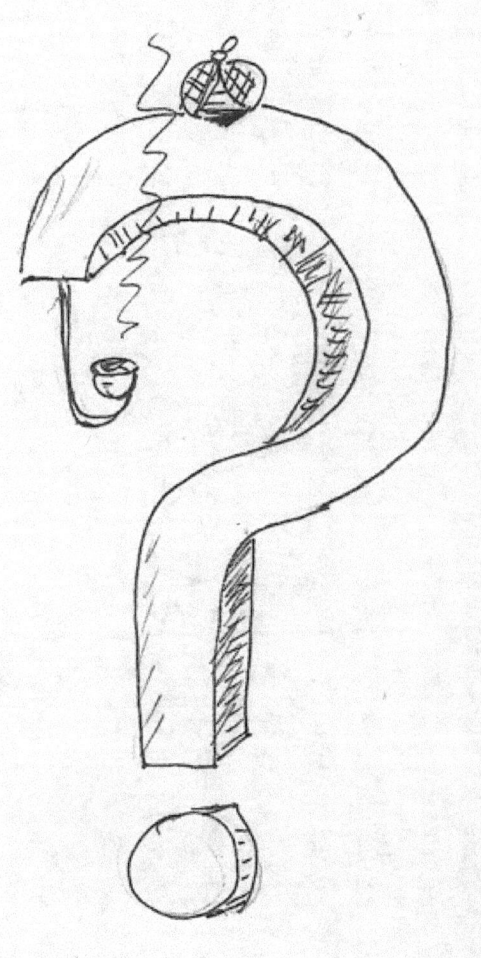

"...There could no longer be any question about it ..."
SIGN

Sherlock Holmes
On Board

"…Well, we took him on board, this man …"   BLAC

Sherlock Holmes
Ten-Point Buck

"...But he was off like a deer..." MUSG

Sherlock Holmes
Pops His Knuckles

"...Did you observe his knuckles? ..."   CREE

Sherlock Holmes
Visits Paris, TX

"...the stately towers of which rose some miles
to our left..." PRIO

Sherlock Holmes
No One's Puppet

"...and all were puppets in his hand..." SOLI

Sherlock Holmes
Cooks a Mean Breakfast

"...we sat together to the excellent breakfast..." BLAC

Sherlock Holmes
Inches Along

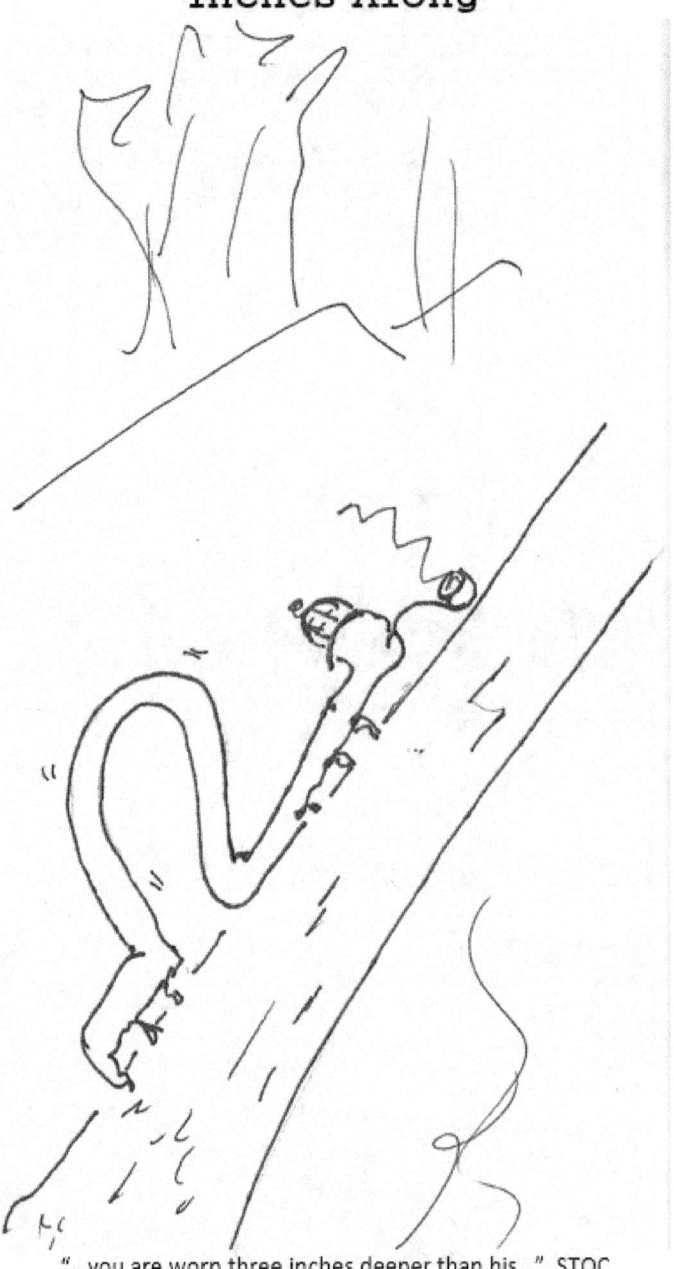

"...you are worn three inches deeper than his..." STOC

Sherlock Holmes
Loves Shark Week

"...want to see my shark..." MAZA

Sherlock Holmes
Disguised as a Wisk-Broom

"...I took a long sweep around..." MAZA

Sherlock Holmes
Enjoys a Jersey Mike's

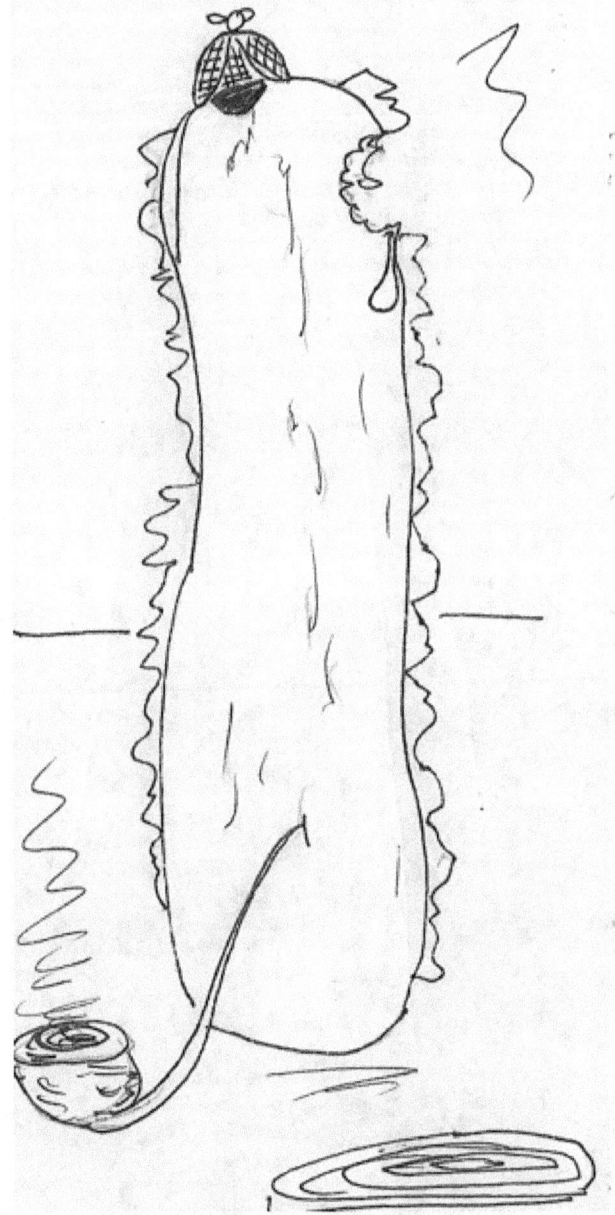

"...devoured sandwiches at irregular hours..." SECO

Sherlock Holmes
Visits Chile

"...South American," I hazarded..." SIGN

Sherlock Holmes
Believes

"...on the most extraordinary matters..." COPP

Sherlock Holmes
Visits Israel

"...in sympthy and tradition...   NAVA

Sherlock Holmes
Enjoys a Street Taco

"...Had you any indication that food was conveyed
from one house to another?..." BLAN

Sherlock Holmes
Fells a Tree

"...The largest tree in the neighbourhood..." BOSC

Sherlock Holmes
Good Oral Hygene

"...it fell over with its keen white teeth..." COPP

195

Sherlock Holmes
Diguised as an Octipus

"...so prolific the creatures seem..." DYIN

Sherlock Holmes
In Hong Kong

"...well, but China?..." REDH

Sherlock Holmes
Just Hanging About

"…was hanging the managing director of the
Franco-Midland Hardware Company…" STOC

198

Sherlock Holmes
Watering his Plants

"...he stumbled over the watering-pot..." DEVI

Sherlock Holmes
Pops a Wheelie

"...In an instant it reared up..." SIGN

Sherlock Holmes
Visits the Rosetta Stone

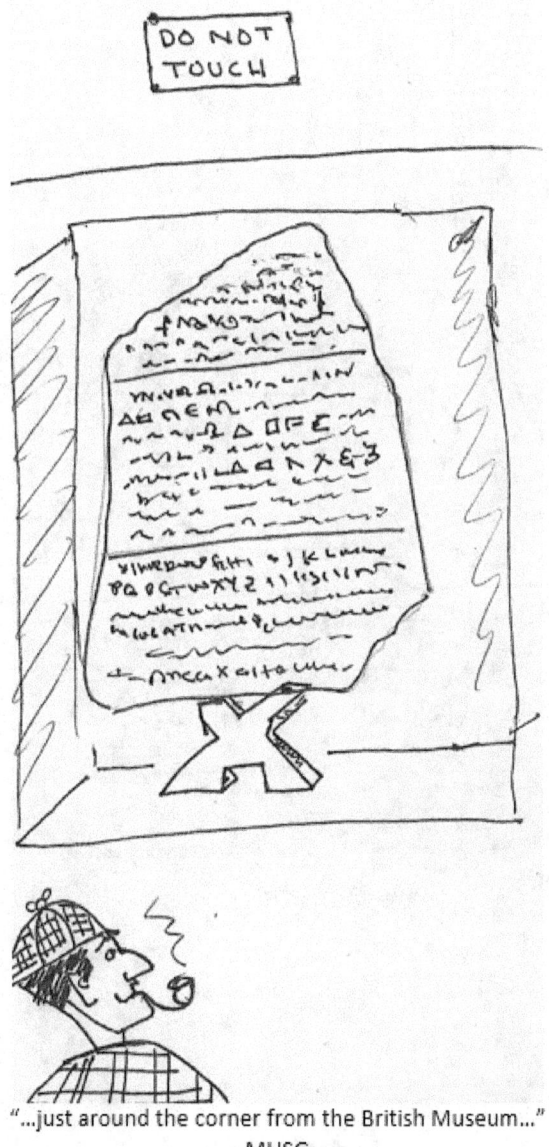

"...just around the corner from the British Museum..."
MUSG

Sherlock Holmes
Inspects an Alfa Romeo

"…The landlord of the Alpha…" BLUE

Sherlock Holmes
Even He Gets the Blues

"...sad story this, sir..." LION

Sherlock Holmes
Calls Heads

"...he had tossed it..." BOSC

Sherlock Holmes
Disguised as a Mermaid

"...as I am a swimmer myself..." LION

Sherlock Holmes
Visits New Zealand

"...You have been in New Zealand..." GLOR

Sherlock Holmes
Phone Home

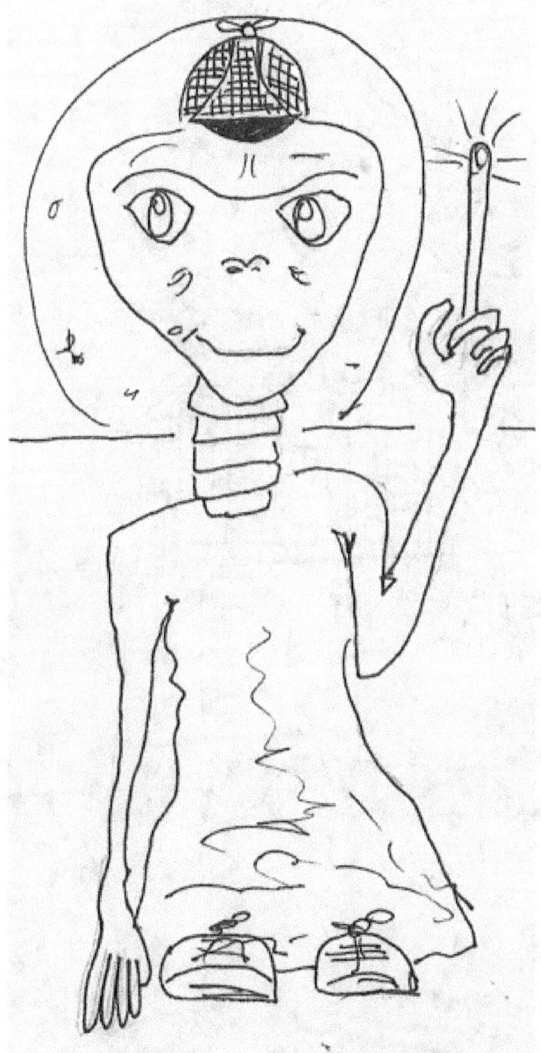

"...The telephone directory lay on the table beside me..." 3GAR

Sherlock Holmes:
It's Just a Scratch

"...it's nothing Holmes. It's a mere scratch..." 3GAR

Sherlock Holmes:
Baritsu Black Belt

"...I have some knowledge of Bartisu..." EMPT

Sherlock Holmes:
Explores Mars

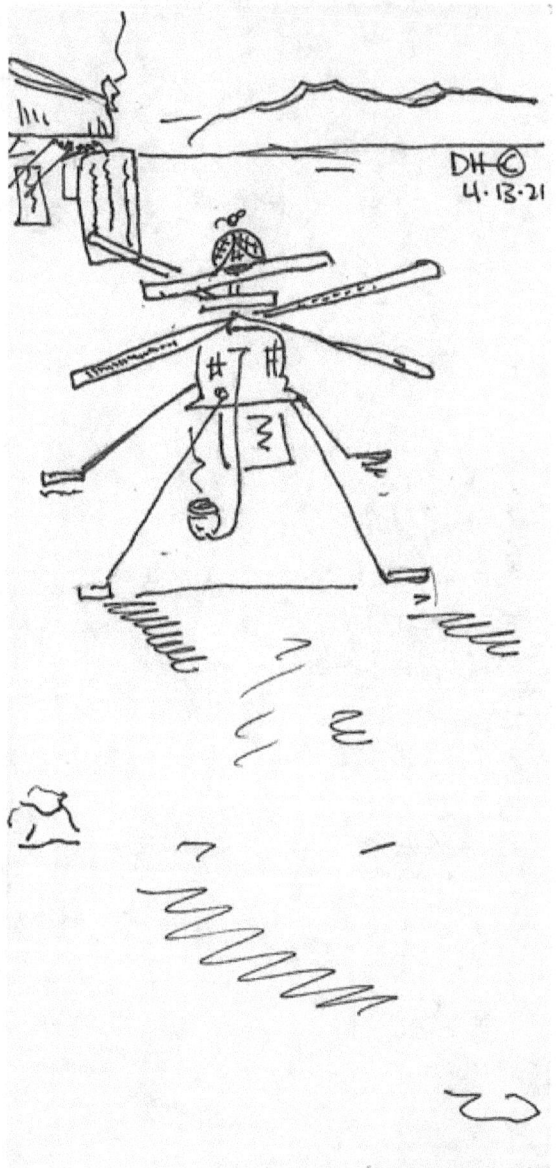

"...will in itself justify a man's life on this planet..."
EMPT

Sherlock Holmes:
Visits Space-X

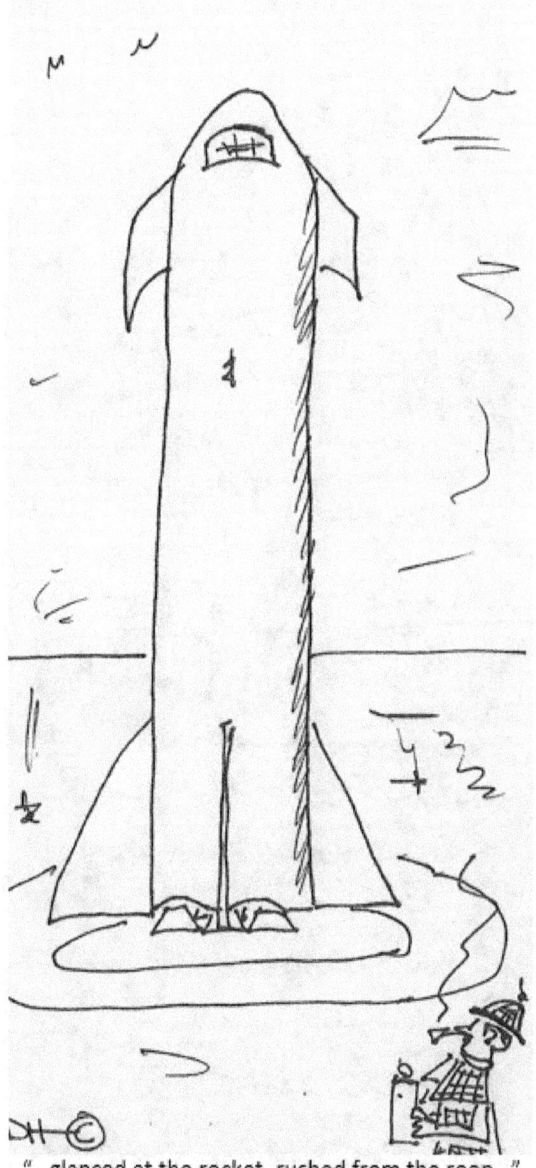

"...glanced at the rocket, rushed from the roon..."
SCAN

Sherlock Holmes:
Too Cool for the Pool

"...he lies beside the water-pool and waits..."
BLAC

Sherlock Holmes
Never Uses a Net

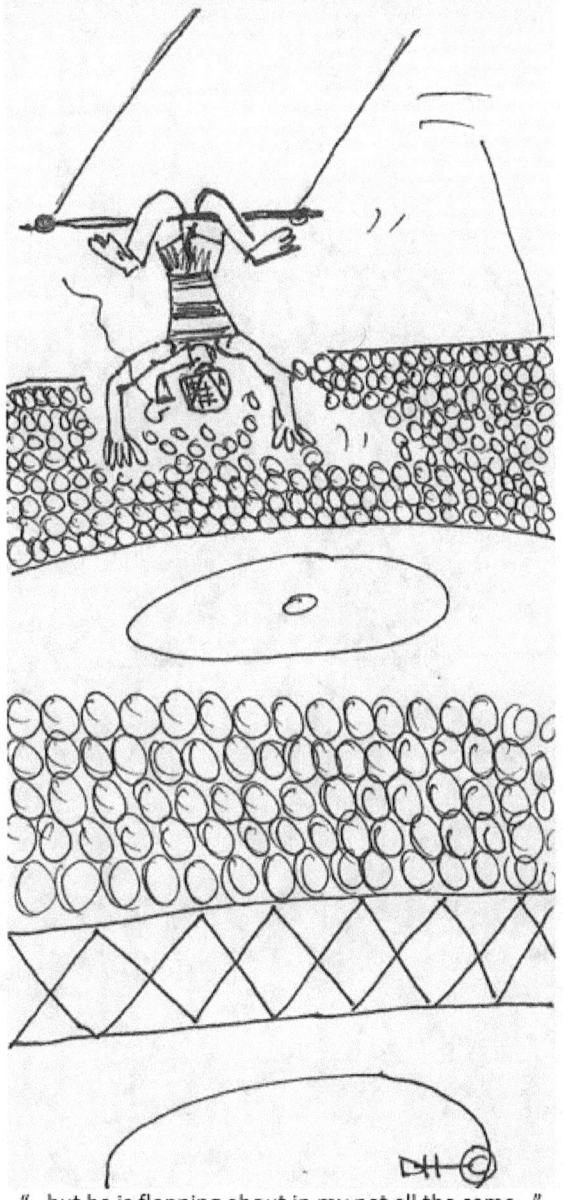

"...but he is flopping about in my net all the same..."
MAZA

Sherlock Holmes
In His Flying Suit

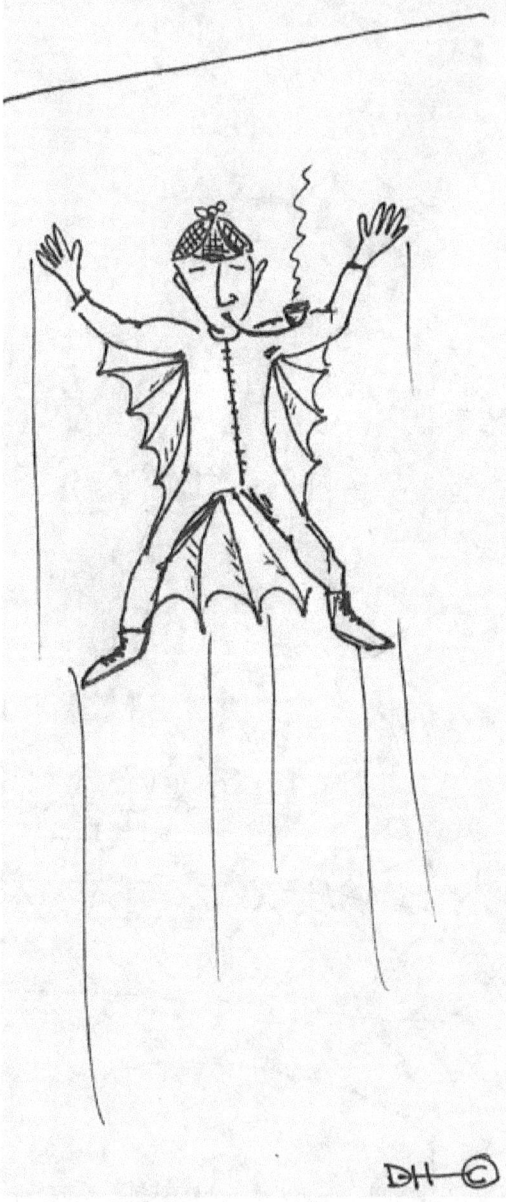

"...a wild thrill as this mad flying-man..." SIGN

Sherlock Holmes
The Problem of Thor's Bridge

"...we are now on the bridge..." SIGN

Sherlock Holmes
Enjoys a Dr Pepper

"...And a whisky and a soda?..." SIGN

Sherlock Holmes
Cleans the Gutters

"...even if he had come from the gutter..." ILLU

Sherlock Holmes: National Symbol?

"...high-nosed, eagle eyed..." SECO

Sherlock Holmes Working as a Parking Meter

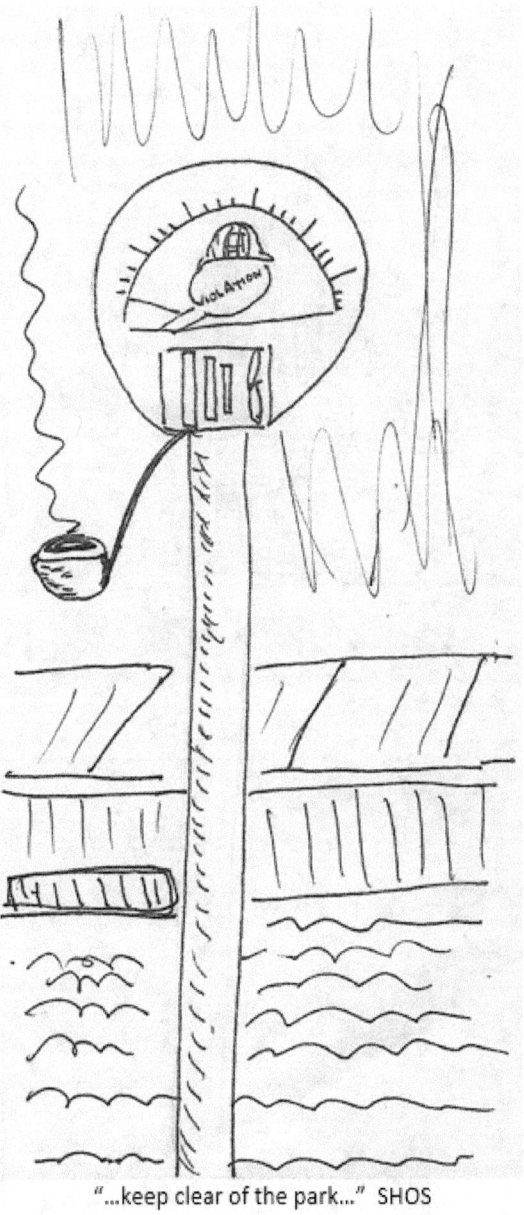

"...keep clear of the park..." SHOS

Sherlock Holmes
Needs to Pee

"...that's what the flags are for..." STUD

Sherlock Holmes
Neanderthal Man

"...showed traces of the ancient people..." HOUN